PASS of the CROW

I Am Currency II

Whitney L. Grady (signature)

Whitney L. Grady

Amazing Things Press

Book and cover design by Julie L. Casey

ISBN 978-0692496282
Printed in the United States of America.

For more information, visit
www.amazingthingspress.com

For Mom and Dad

who couldn't have known

that the barefoot summers outside

and the kisses goodnight

and the sacrifices made to give

three little girls the world

would give me the power

to travel through time

and across oceans

at the tip of my pencil

1

Blue

Where was she? Nevel's scarred hands were cupped over his brow in search of her. Two distinct scars now marked his right hand: on the tender web of thin skin between his thumb and his index finger, a scar began as straight as an arrow running up towards his wrist—a result of Quinn's knife slice at one of his attempted outback escapes; the other scar was just to the left of his arrow scar and looked like a sunburst— a souvenir from the cop's cigarette. Both were no longer scabs, but healed wounds—scars from months before. His eyes scanned across the blue ripples of the sea. Too much time had passed. Nevel's breaths were short, his chest felt tight. Without her, he didn't stand a chance.

The winds were light, but cool and Nevel ran the flats of his palms up and down along his biceps with quick friction for warmth. The Australian winters Nevel remembered before the MegaCrash—when a huge meteor smashed into the earth, destroying most of modern civilization—were the add-one-blanket-to-the-bed kind of cold, maybe even put on a pair of socks, but after the MegaCrash the seasons could be quite unpredictable. The patchwork rag pants and the thin shirt he wore—his city attire—did little to protect him from the current and perhaps temporary chill. He paced up and down the beach, his boots sliding on the uneven sand as it gave way to his weight. There were no shells: no butterfly-wing casings that had once housed mussels, no segmented and bumpy patterned fan molds pressed in sand, no fossilized rock with tubular casts. Nevel knew why the beach was void of shells. Though he hadn't summered on the Gold Coast, he had read plenty about the shell-covered beaches of the past. Now the city dwellers were shell seekers, leaving no prize behind. Nevel had a book shelved in the library in his mind called *The Beach-Combers Guide to Shell Identification*. In his earlier trips to this beach since his time in the city, he had hoped to stumble upon a beaded periwinkle, a lion's paw, or a lightning whelk. Now he knew better than to look to the sand for treasures; they had all been stripped.

Nevel could not swim. Growing up on the outskirts of the outback without any water nearby other than the occasional shallow creek did little to instill swimming as a boyhood trait. Beyond the bathtub,

Nevel's experiences with swimming were minimal. He didn't dare get in the water here for fear of drowning. He paced, stamping his worn hiking boots in damp sand along the water's edge. He was trapped by a border of water he could not penetrate. With every blue wave that licked the shore, his heart beat faster and he paced in rhythm. The moments were critical. Nevel could hear his own heart beating in his chest like the sounds of a ticking clock. Tick. Tick. The sounds grew louder and louder. Like approaching thunder, the sounds strengthened and began to shake his very soul. Tick. Tick. Every second counted. Blue water extended to blue sky in the horizon. Squinting and scanning, Nevel did not see her.

The rhythmic, monotonous swells taunted him, taking their time to slowly billow and grow, then curl and rise, before rushing forward and finally bursting with froth and spray. Each wave that perfectly and strategically formed marked time that passed—time he did not have. The waves erased each of his pacing footprints, proving how fruitless they were. Still he paced and kept his eyes on the great blue, impermeable sea.

The insatiable patterns that rippled from sea to sky and back to sea again began to almost hypnotize Nevel. His mind flashed back to their arrival in Brisbane so many months before.

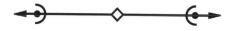

"Ready for our adventure, Bookkeeper?" Quinn

whispered into Nevel's ear as she followed him off the train. Nevel turned around to smile back at her and offer his hand to help her step down the iron train steps and into the city of Brisbane. Quinn was stunning, cloaked in the steam from the black iron horse that had delivered them as she stepped down onto the platform. She was wearing the navy dress with a white-piped, scalloped edge that trimmed the hem just above her kneecaps and framed her slender neck and long arms at the capped sleeves. Their visit to a puddle before boarding the train had washed the red clay dirt from her exposed skin on her arms and legs and face, but her long red hair was unruly despite the numerous times she combed through it with her fingers on their ride here. Her wide, green eyes looked left and right, taking in her surroundings as they stood on the busy platform. Nevel took in his surroundings as well. Train conductors blew silver whistles that hung around their necks on navy cords that matched their uniforms. Dozens of people moved left and right, bobbing their heads up and down from behind a long, red fence about twenty feet from the tracks, their faces hopeful as they all used wide, scrutinizing eyes to rake through the faces of the train's arrivals. Some people disembarking the train ran to the arms of loved ones and they hugged with arms reaching through the spokes of the red fence barrier. Others quietly walked by the gated crowd, nodding at the recognition of their greeter before strolling coolly on to the baggage area. The people with whom they had ridden the train were all dressed to the nines. Surely they were political, Nevel thought; only government representatives and their relatives had the kind of knowledge, and therefore the currency, to get train tickets. Their welcomers had clearly tried to match the occasion with their oversized hats, brass buttoned suits, and painted faces. In this day and age, wealth and status were expressed through physical appearance. Vanity was highly regarded. Nevel looked down at himself nervously, concerned he may not fit in. He barely recognized the man he had become. His fresh khaki pants were his, but the white collared button-down shirt was his father's, a shirt his dad usually pulled out once a year to please his wife at her birthday dinner in the back yard. Last year, the clothes would have billowed loosely around Nevel's thin frame. Now, his arms were tight muscle and filled the cavern of the sleeves. His stomach was hard and flat, his thighs thick and strong— all improvements due to the life of a young man on the run from the government. Nevel flattened his hands against his stomach, ironing out the wrinkles from travel, before crouching a moment to retie the freed lace on his right boot. Standing tall again, he looked at Quinn who also had been taking in the crowds. He tightened the straps to the pack he wore on his back and Quinn leaned back to be sure it was closed and secure. What his father had packed for them was all they had heading into this new city and they both wanted to make sure it was secure. Nevel offered Quinn his hand and she accepted it with a smile. There would be no one behind the red fence to greet them, but that did not bother Nevel at all. He had Quinn. Nevel thought about the fact that they stood, hand in hand, in a city where no one knew their past;

not his bookkeeper status, not their trial and escape from execution, not their rank in society. Here, they could be anyone. He took a deep breath and filled his lungs, gathering his gumption before looking again at his partner. They shared a grin between them. Quinn squeezed Nevel's hand twice before excitedly pulling Nevel with her toward the train station exit.

The excitement wore off quickly as Quinn and Nevel stepped not ten feet through the exit gates of the station to watch the elite dash off in horse-drawn buggies and suddenly realize where they had been left. As the dust settled from the last buggy's departure, nothing remained but piles of horse manure, a few lingering hisses of the parked train, and the clinking of the closed gate the train conductors were locking behind them. What lay before them was a city that immediately taught Nevel the contrast between the light, country life of Morgan Creek and the dark, dingy city streets of Brisbane.

"It's not how I remembered," Quinn said as her smile washed from her face and her wide eyes narrowed in disappointment. Nevel shared in her surprise. Life beyond the station looked like a scene from Gotham City in Nevel's library's comic book collection. It was a picture of urban decay. Looming skyscrapers with broken windows and leaning towers were void of life after the first few floors. The city streets and sidewalks were flowing with a sea of ragged, lost people who appeared more like scavenging rats than humans to Nevel. Quinn shivered a bit and Nevel wrapped his arm around her to warm her exposed skin. A cool blanket of gray hung over the city and light winds tossed Quinn's already unruly red locks, adding the only splash of color against the backdrop of gray that Nevel could see.

"The river should be just beyond the buildings, it's beautiful—" Quinn's hopeful reminiscing was cut short by a woman in rags stomping past.

"Stay away from the river if you know what's good for ya!" the woman warned in a huff. "Tourists!"

"What do you think?" Quinn looked at Nevel.

"I imagine a lot has changed, Quinn. I'm sure the river is polluted, filled with bacteria from a city without sewage or plumbing or—"

Quinn cut Nevel short. "Never mind, Nevel, I get it. Let's just get on with it." She stared at the city ahead.

2

City

From the edge of the train station, a long street stretched and narrowed between the tall buildings indefinitely. It reminded Nevel of pen and ink cityscapes he had studied in his art books and he couldn't help but open the book in his mind. "Directions: In order for the artist to create space with 3D tactics, to bring out depth perception and, therefore, a realistic view, the artist should use a ruler to bring lines from a single point in the distance out at a span. Along the lines, buildings should be drawn smaller closer to the vortex and larger at the front of the page. A city street that appears to stretch on forever in the distance will develop from it." Nevel closed the book and looked at the scene before him. Indeed they were the same.

8

"Shall we?" Nevel invited Quinn who still stared in shock.

"Why not?" Quinn said and with a deep breath, she took a step toward the city.

The city wasn't exactly as Nevel had expected either. There was no rhyme or reason to the life of this city as there had been in Morgan Creek. In Morgan Creek, the streets showed people at work, in trade, on their way to or from school or shopping. Here, it wasn't clear what all of these wandering people were doing on the streets. With the exception of the trading posts that were set up every block or so, people didn't seem to be working or playing; they merely seemed to be existing.

The city buildings were run-down, used only on the bottom few floors as living quarters. There were no formal stores set up with glyphs on the windows showing what sort of trade they were interested in like in Morgan Creek. Nevel worried how trading would work in this city. On Brary Day every year, the only day that ordinary citizens were allowed to enter the libraries and have access to books, the streets of Morgan Creek were set up with rudimentary bartering posts. He guessed it was like this every day in the city.

The first trading post they passed was a long bench stacked with household-type items: colorless balls of yarn spun of an animal fur Nevel didn't recognize, stacks of patches of cloth reinvented from old sheets and blankets and upholstery, and bits of wire and shells. Two girls who couldn't have been more than twelve manned the post. Quinn immediately walked up to them with kind eyes.

9

"What kinda knowin' you ladies after?" Quinn cheerfully asked.

"We's after planting ideas," a freckle-faced girl in rags said, "or a bit 'bout curing these coughs." As if on cue, her partner at the other end of the bench, a blond girl in pigtails, started coughing uncontrollably. Quinn stared and Nevel interjected in an attempt to help.

He leaned in to the freckle-faced girl and quietly shared, "You got any eucalyptus around here?"

"Sometimes. We trade a lady near the station with our knowin' on the cloth bits, how to turn 'em to good yarn. She brings stuff from the countryside. We can get it from her." The girl was looking at Nevel intensely now, ready to accept the new knowledge as currency, checking over her shoulder to be sure that it wouldn't spill over to anyone else. She motioned for Nevel to lean in even closer.

He did, whispering in her ear, "You boil the eucalyptus in a pot of water, hold a sheet over your sister's head and over the pot. Let her breath in the steam a couple times a day. It'll help."

"Right, thank you, sir. Take a bit of rag and wire for your knowin'."

Nevel gladly grabbed two patches of cloth and a stretch of wire and nodded his thanks. He didn't have to worry much about the little girls wondering where he got his knowledge. It was an easy trade, one he felt good about because he knew he had helped a sick little girl.

"Where's your band?" The blond asked between coughs as Nevel started to walk away. She pointed at his sleeve. Nevel didn't know what she meant. "And your mask?"

"My what?" Nevel asked, but the coughing took over before the girl could answer. The freckle-faced girl put her arm around the blond and patted her on the back to soothe her.

"Star here! City's finest news! Bit a 'knowin'll getcha a read of The Star!" A heavy woman with missing teeth held up a folded yellowed piece of paper with light ink on it just a block away. Her voice was so loud, it captured Nevel and Quinn's attention and they moved toward her.

"We've got to get a paper!" Quinn said as they walked toward the woman whose barter post was nothing more than a stack of crates in the middle of the dirty street. Nevel knew Quinn was right; they had to get a paper. It would be their best bet to figure out this place. He knew, though, that he would have to be careful in his trade with an adult.

The woman had a stack of only about a dozen papers. Nevel figured they probably were made once a month and wouldn't be of worth to the poor folks, probably just another luxury for the political personalities to pat themselves on the back about their good fortunes in comparison to the dirt poor in this modern age. Nevel wondered if the schools here even taught poor city kids to read or if the focus was more on survival classes. Nevel was happy the schools of Morgan Creek taught both fundamentals like reading and math as well as the more highly sought after survival classes. Nevel wondered about how the papers were made. Morgan Creek did not have a paper; the town

11

was small enough that everybody knew everything they needed to know just by word of mouth and the occasional postings in town. He imagined the high government officials here dictated to the newspaper what it wanted in print and the paper tediously inked it and pressed copies to sell in small supplies. Really, it didn't matter; all Nevel knew was a newspaper in a city that was unknown to him would serve as a wealth of information.

"I got a trade for knowin'," Nevel said to the woman who seemed surprised to see him standing before her.

"Yeah? What kinda knowin'?" she asked skeptically, looking him up and down and staring at his arm and then back at his face like the little blond had done. She then coughed into the corner of her arm at her elbow and Nevel was instantly relieved that she too had the cough that so many others in this city had.

Nevel figured if the last trade had worked, it might just work again here, but this time he may have to be prepared to defend it. "I got a bit to help the cough."

The woman perked up a bit at this, but then tested him. "How you know somethin' I don't already know?" She looked now at Quinn, taking in her fancy dress and rolling her eyes.

"Just came into town. My Pop is a doc back home. Government sent us here to help out for a few days."

This seemed to do the trick. The lady lifted an apron tied round her wide, lumpy waist and pulled out a logbook. She pulled a writing quill from the gray bun that sat atop her head. She licked the tip and then dipped it in an ink sac that hung around her belt before leaning in to log the currency she was about to accept. She leaned so close to Nevel that he had to hold his breath against her heinous body odor.

Nevel quickly shared the bit about the eucalyptus and then leaned back to take a breath. Her grin showed dark, rotting teeth and a few holes where teeth had previously been. She scribbled and nodded and then handed him the paper.

He tucked it under his arm for safe keeping, nodded his thanks as she glared at him and spit on the ground between coughs, and then they moved on quickly through the crowds.

The buildings they walked by obviously used to house businesses. Nevel read their previous titles as he passed them. The faded stone etching of the Farmer's Mercantile Bank and Trust was legible, but barely. The marquis dangling on the side of a building that read JA_ESVI_LE FU_NIT_R_ made him think a bit before guessing what it had been. Nevel imagined the "M" falling and killing an unsuspecting passerby on a day like any other. He winced at the thought of a furniture store, which surely used to invite happy, growing families to furnish their city homes with loveseats and four poster beds, playing the role of murderer in this new era.

The buildings were now clearly the homes of these city-dwellers. People stood at their broken windows looking out with blank stares. Children sat lifelessly on the sidewalks in front of their homes poking at the bugs that crawled eerily about. The sounds on the streets were monotone, like the background to a creepy movie Nevel and Quinn were watching in short clips as they walked past, looking inside the broken windows that exposed the squats these city folks called home. Squawking chickens were loose inside many of the makeshift homes. Smoke billowed from windows as the residents tried to cook inside.

Every now and then, Nevel could see a sliver of the river between buildings, but it was lifeless and dark. He imagined the beauty it had surely once offered; what a pity that it now teemed with waste and disease. Almost every person they passed was either coughing or sickly-looking with hollow eyes. Many children inside the homes were crying. There was no music, no laughter, no joy. The sounds of desperation, coughs and moans and cries, were deafening. It was as if these people were all waiting to be saved, but by whom?

They stopped when a slow parade came around a corner. It wasn't the type of parade Nevel remembered before the MegaCrash: no trumpets or fanfare or brightly-colored costumes. This parade was dark and somber. Its members hung their heads and a slow, sad tune spilled from their lips. As they walked, people on the street moved out of their way, stopped, and hung their heads as well. As it grew closer, Nevel finally realized why. The marchers pulled a cart between them, on which lay a small wooden box draped with a dark cloth. This was no parade; it was a funeral. The small box surely held a lifeless child. The tears running down the sickly faces of the family walking alongside the box showed the depth of their sorrow. Nevel hung his head, as did Quinn, as the funeral party marched by.

"Let's go," Nevel said to Quinn as the parade passed. He headed in the opposite direction, knowing they couldn't just stand and stare. They would have to make some sense of this place and Nevel knew the only way to get started would be to immerse themselves in this God-forsaken place, whether he wanted to or not.

"Go where?" Quinn asked, throwing her hands up, still stupefied by her surroundings. Nevel imagined she had seen this city in its glory and figured it might be more difficult for her to take in as her expectations would have been much higher than Nevel's.

"Don't know yet, but I am sure we'll figure it out," Nevel tried to reassure Quinn as he pulled her further into the foreboding metropolis.

It quickly became clear to both Nevel and Quinn that their steps on the cold, broken city cement had to be deliberate to keep their forward momentum. "Spare a 'bit 'a bread?" a coughing grey-haired woman begged from the soiled sheets she crouched under on the sidewalk, her reaching upturned hand crusted in blood and grime. Nevel pulled the staring Quinn to the right and onto the asphalt street, but there they were met again with the city's grasping hands. "Bit 'a knowin' will get ya' labor" a toothless thin man who appeared to be at death's door barked. His words were interrupted by his coughs, which he caught in his elbow, but the coughs didn't deter him from his goal to make a trade. He coughed into one arm and held the other arm up to present what appeared to be his young, emaciated six or seven-year-old son. Nevel swallowed his disgust and pulled Quinn back onto the sidewalk and they moved on, Nevel hoping he could just look up to the sky so as not to store these sad images in the vault of his mind. Above the crowded streets, he saw nothing but chalky scribblings at the tops of the vacant skyscrapers, apparently markings from the government patrol with signs of skulls and crosses to warn of death, despair, and disease. They moved forward, sweaty palm in sweaty palm, fearing this new world. Nevel drowned out the sounds of beggars by humming *Advance Australia Fare* in his mind, disregarding every beggar who bumped into them on purpose to feel for something to steal, keeping focus to check on Quinn every few moments, but otherwise eyes up and out of the way of the view of the desperation that was this city.

"Where will we go?" Quinn asked Nevel in a whisper as she leaned into his ear, still continuing to walk aimlessly. For a girl who had easily survived the wilds of the outback, the capture by Driscoll's raucous crew, and the escape from their corrupt government, Quinn seemed to be surprisingly uneasy in these surroundings.

"We'll figure it out," Nevel replied under his breath with his chin tucked to his chest as he watched his feet move on. He stopped a moment and looked around before whispering in Quinn's ear, "I think it's fair to say we know we aren't stopping here."

"Yeah, I'd take Shanty Town over this place any day," Quinn said with conviction, and they walked on, from sidewalk to street, and onto the sidewalk again, avoiding beggars and piles of waste and potholes.

Here and there they would have to walk around an old pot or an old trashcan filled with dirt in an attempt to grow food, but few had sprouts and even the sprouts appeared lifeless like the city-dwellers.

"Notice anything odd, Bookkeeper?" Quinn quietly asked Nevel. They stopped on the edge of the busy street and both were taking it all in. Nevel felt eyes on him and it made him nervous to stop and chat.

"I notice a lot that's odd," Nevel said. He didn't want to stop and gab about it, though. He didn't know where they were going, but he figured anywhere had to be better than here. "We've got to keep moving, Quinn." He pulled at her hand to get her walking again. She appeared so distracted, staring at every dirty face as if she were studying them. Nevel couldn't look at the faces; their faces made them real, gave them stories of heartache and loss. Nevel didn't want empathy to take hold and distract him from his task. It was clear Quinn was already distracted. If there was something Nevel had learned since the outback, it was that survival takes focus. Right now, though they weren't in the wild, they still had to survive. Glancing from the cracked black asphalt beneath his feet to the crowded streets and tall buildings, he felt his first twinge of homesickness. It wasn't so much for his parents; he missed them, but he had faith he would see them or at least hear from them again. Nevel missed the wild of his country, the red dirt, the trees and brush, the wide-open spaces. He wanted to be back in the outback with Quinn by a fire eating meat they had hunted. He felt trapped in this concrete jungle, like a bird in a cage.

17

"It's almost all women and children," Quinn quietly called ahead as she stepped faster to keep up with Nevel who was now ahead of her, no longer by her side but pulling her urgently through the streets by her hand.

Nevel stopped and brought his eyes up from the pavement. They were moving through the same crowds, but for the first time Nevel saw his surroundings differently. Finally he noticed what Quinn had pointed out: women and girls manned every bartering post; women were the ones begging; women held the hands or kept the watch over the children in the streets; women and girls stood blankly at the broken windows looking out; with only the exception of a few very old and sickly men here and there, Nevel found himself in a city of females. It didn't make sense to Nevel. Where were the men?

3

Library

Quinn and Nevel walked further into the city. The more they became enveloped by the predominantly female crowds, the more they realized how much Nevel was beginning to stand out in them.

"We aren't even seeing police," Quinn murmured. The air filled with an unbearable stench. She covered her mouth and nose with her hand. Nevel turned his face into the collar of his shirt. Trash and grime covered the streets. Foul odors permeated the air.

"There have gotta be men around here somewhere," Nevel said quietly scanning his newly suspicious surroundings with more keen perception. Quinn jumped as she narrowly avoided a chicken that quickly ran between her feet. Nevel smiled at her and she gave him a look as if to dare him to make a joke about her awkward footing.

They walked on, side by side again, still holding hands while both constantly scanned their surroundings. The cracks in the leaning buildings along their path were very telling—they were as unsafe as these city streets—but something every few steps caught Nevel's eye. Or did it? Nevel couldn't decide if shadows and reflections on the window glass high above were playing tricks on his eyes or if he was seeing figures watching the streets from above. Nevel made a conscious effort to walk and appear to be looking straight ahead, but he kept his peripheral view open and soaked in every detail from the windows above. Nevel was reminded of the feeling of being followed by an ever-present moon during his journey through the outback as now he felt eyes following him from above. Nevel didn't know if it was one person passing through the buildings and following him, or if there were dozens of eyes above watching everyone. Nevel paid close attention to the next building he approached on his right. The protruding signage and grandiose architecture led Nevel to believe it was an old theater of some sort. Surely it had once been full of music and glamorous people, but now it was void of any life—including spying eyes. Nevel looked at the buildings to the left. He imagined these were most likely old business offices as they were stacked in rudimentary form reaching to the sky in their sleek and organized stature. These too, were lifeless. As he passed them, Nevel stopped and looked back over his shoulder at the old theater on the right that had been void of life moments before. His eyes locked on another's in a high balcony window. His heart skipped a beat. A man in the shadows held his stare for only a moment before quickly disappearing into the dark building.

Walking on, Nevel now noticed a change in the atmosphere. The chalky marks of distress dissolved from the sides of buildings and in their place began to appear flags Nevel recognized— those that had once made him shudder—with an iron fist over a book. Now, their familiarity made them oddly comforting. Buildings were stark and utilitarian, not unkempt and chaotic like the squats they had passed closer to the train station. Nevel and Quinn walked to the center of this city block and stopped, taking in the different surroundings.

It was clear that the bottom few floors of several buildings acted as residences, but the windows were not all broken and exposed like the ones further back. These windows didn't reveal sickly families through broken glass in their one dirty room where they were smashed in like sardines with animals and sheets separating one squat from the next. Instead, each dwelling had boards covering all of the windows but one or two. The boards were ornamental and had beautiful designs that appeared to have been hammered into intricate stars, basket weaves, and quilted patterns. Several showed the image of the fist over the book. Shells were worked into many of the patterns. The windows without boards had all the broken glass taken out and had dozens of strings hanging at varying lengths with broken glass pieces hanging at the ends.

The varying lengths allowed the light in but kept privacy as the glass pieces blew in the wind and sang like wind chimes and reflected light like prisms. These windows showed just a small bit of the dwellings when the wind blew just right, exposing a woman at a wooden table folding clothing or a child playing on the floor while a mother knitted in a chair. These dwellings were much larger and did not seem to be as cramped. Several had wire cages hanging in boardless windows where birds were more sanitarily housed away from the humans. Other windows housed small gardens that grew in crates perching on the windowsills, some trellised to help tomato vines climb.

Not only was the physical appearance of the surroundings changing, but the crowds themselves seemed to change as well. The beggars stayed back. The people here, still mainly women and children, were cleaner and well dressed. Their eyes were dark and hollow and their lips straight-lined. They were more purposeful than the lingering beggars a few blocks back. These people were busy living: harvesting eggs and tomatoes from window crates, sweeping, sewing, grinding seed. Quinn looked down at her feet and Nevel looked to see if she was standing in waste as they had narrowly avoided doing so several times on their walk so far. He was surprised that the broken asphalt beneath their feet was not quite so littered with waste. Perhaps this was why Quinn was looking down, surprised by the sudden improvements. Nevel breathed in and Quinn did the same, both smiled with a sigh of relief. The raunchy smells had dissipated. Though the city remained dark in atmosphere, here things seemed better.

"There they are," Nevel pointed inconspicuously to a line of about two dozen uniformed men standing guard around a building at the corner of the city block. Their uniforms were just like those of police officers before the MegaCrash, navy with gold bars on the sleeves and brass buttons on the coats over long navy slacks. Nevel assumed they were still using the same uniforms today as no better option could be crafted and in such great quantity with today's resources.

"Well, that can't be all the men this city has," Quinn said with her hands on her hips.

The building the officers surrounded was much prettier than the ones they had passed on their long walk so far today. It was not a skyscraper like so many of the others and was made of very old grey stone. The low slate roof was covered in pigeons. A large tree with a knotty trunk at least five feet wide stood at the left corner of the lot the building occupied, oblivious to its location in a city of concrete. Nevel stared at the tree. Its bushy green leaves were waving in the wind from the long twisty branches. He missed his pear tree in his back yard at home. Under this particular tree was a small patch of grass with a border of wildflowers that had the prettiest yellow hue. The tree was so grand; it almost stole the attention from the beautiful old building with which it shared the lot. Finally, Nevel's eyes reluctantly left the tree and fell upon the building. The building's stones were woven in a pattern that came to fruition in a grand arch over the enormous doors. The doors must have been twelve feet tall, made of wooden planks that were flanked by wide strips of black iron and large, round iron nail heads. Nevel read the signage on the door: PUBLIC LIBRARY.

Nevel took it in as if he were looking at Michelangelo's *David*. It actually took his breath away. Nevel had read many books and stored them in the library in his mind, perhaps even some books from this very library, but he knew there were hundreds, maybe thousands more within this building that he may have never had the pleasure of seeing. He wondered what they were and longed to get inside.

"Isn't it somethin'?" Quinn said looking at the library and then at Nevel. "Betcha want to get inside." Quinn's hands were still on her hips and she was twisting back and forth, looking from Nevel to the library and back to Nevel again. "Don't get any wild ideas; we've got a job to do," she said, poking Nevel teasingly in the side with her elbow.

"Ha, yeah, I know," Nevel replied, but still he couldn't take his eyes off of the building.

"Where do you suppose we go from here, Nevel?" Quinn was looking left and right, surveying the area as Nevel did the same.

"From the looks of it," Nevel said as he scanned the city block, "this is the safest area we've seen."

"Cleanest too," Quinn added.

"That's got to be the police station," Quinn whispered as she motioned with her eyes to the bottom floor of a looming skyscraper with government flags hanging at every window and old lampposts on the stoop in front of it. A uniformed guard stood at either side of the door.

Nevel squinted his eyes to try to read the sign that hung above the door. "I think it says Police Post Thirty Two," Nevel said.

"You thinking what I'm thinking?" Quinn asked Nevel as they both looked at the dark, empty windows far above the station. He knew it might be stupid, making the floors high above a police station their hideout until they could figure out their next move, but Nevel also knew that in many of the mysteries he read in the library in his mind, sometimes hiding in plain sight was the best hiding place of all.

The residents of this city, he had surmised from their journey from the train station, resided only on the first few floors of these monstrous buildings. He figured the higher floors must be off limits since the MegaCrash: too much instability, too difficult to get to and from without elevators, too far from water and waste dumping.

Nevel nodded at Quinn's suggestion and they walked casually past the police station and around the block.

The alley beyond the station was not very populated. Two young children kicked a ball made of tied rags in the street, probably brother and sister, Nevel assumed, as a woman who looked to be their mother walked aimlessly a few steps ahead of them toward town. A few horses stood in makeshift street stalls created with old chain fencing. Nevel knew they belonged to police by the monogrammed blankets on their backs. He couldn't help but be enamored by the beautiful beasts. Nevel reached his hand out to touch the velvety nose of a brown mare that tossed her sandy brown mane and swished her tail in excitement. Nevel laughed a bit at the horse's call for attention and as he patted the mare's neck, the horse nuzzled him. It made Nevel miss his dog Tank, so he quickly dropped his hand and returned to the task of taking in his surroundings. There were no other people. The street dead-ended at a concrete wall, which Nevel assumed was the back end of an old factory of some sort. The building to the left housed a basket shop that opened only from the front street from which they had just come. There were no doors on this side, only a few windows that were half-boarded and half-open, exposing the stacks and stacks of baskets blocking the view inside. The building to the right was the police station. The horses standing in their stalls at this side of the police station whinnied. Beyond the horses there were a few stacked blue barrels, but nothing else along the street. At the back of the street and along the side of the police station hung an old fire escape that started near a boarded window ledge and reached to the roof. Nevel put his hand up again to pet another horse and continued taking visual inventory. Quinn followed suit and petted the soft white nose of the chestnut mare.

"Only way to go is up," she quietly said as she stroked the horse's nose and smiled as a patrolling officer walked across the main street opening and glanced down at them dismissively for a second before walking out of view again.

"Now!" Nevel signaled and the two ran to the window at the end of the block where the fire escape hung. Nevel boosted Quinn onto the ledge where she nimbly grabbed hold of the black iron and began swiftly flying up it. Nevel easily sprung himself onto the ledge and then up the escape as well. The metal wobbled as they climbed in haste, and Nevel was worried about the amount of noise it was making. Every leap and step clanged and banged as they flew up the metal stairs as fast as they could. The horses whinnied. Nevel held his breath and moved as fast as his body would carry him.

"We've got to get to at least the fifteenth floor," Nevel called up to Quinn in between breaths.

"We're already at ten," Quinn called back. All Nevel could see of her were her long legs swinging up two and three steps at a time, her red hair whipping behind her. Nevel was using the strength of his arms to pull himself up long stretches of the stairs with the railings as he too surged upward. Before he knew it, Quinn launched through a broken window and he followed.

4

Screens

Inside they fell onto a dirty, glass covered floor. Catching her breath and pulling herself up to sit, Quinn asked, "Think anyone saw us?"

Nevel was checking his body for scrapes from the glass as he brushed himself off and got up to look carefully out the window they had just jumped through.

"I can't believe it. No one's down there. No one seemed to see us," he said as he stepped back into the room and looked to Quinn before looking around at his newest surroundings. "You ok?" he asked as he watched her pick a piece of glass from her right calf.

"Oh yeah, just a scratch, mate." Quinn grinned and got up, shaking off her dress and tying her hair into a knot on top of her head.

"Look at this place," Nevel said, taking in his surroundings. They were clearly in an old office building from years ago. Cubicles and desks filled the space, most fallen down and laying on the floor, but some were actually still upright with items on them that Nevel hadn't thought about or seen since childhood—screens, keyboards, telephones—all like antiques in a museum sitting under thick grey dust—dead, silent, still. Quinn walked over to one of the few upright desks and gingerly poked her index finger at a key on the keyboard.

"Scared it's gonna bite?" Nevel asked her as he laughed at her caution and walked to where she stood to get a closer look.

"Amazing," Quinn said in a hushed voice. "It's like a dream. This stuff seems familiar, but I don't really remember; it's been so long."

"We were just kids," Nevel said as he picked up the receiver of a phone that sat on one of the upright desks. It was surprisingly heavy and cold and it was bound to its base with a dirty coil that Nevel strung his fingers through, sending grey dust particles into the air like snowflakes. He sneezed into his elbow and then leaned down to let his fingers bounce off the grid of numbered pushbuttons. He picked up the receiver and put it to his ear. "It might as well have been a million years ago," he said and put the receiver back down.

Quinn walked on, kicking at overturned chairs and cubicle pieces in order to make her way across the room. A large rat scampered out from under one of the piles and startled her. Nevel began walking in another direction, also using his feet now to shift items and check for safe places to step.

"What a mess," Nevel said.

"Let's check out the paper," Quinn suggested.

"Yeah, good idea," Nevel agreed and he kicked clear a spot on the floor to sit down. Quinn looked the spot over a few times before sitting. Nevel assumed she was making sure she wasn't about to sit on a rat. Nevel unfolded the crinkly page and Quinn leaned in over his shoulder to see it. The way the sun shone in through the front windows in the afternoon light made it easy to see the paper from where they sat.

The issue of *The Star* was one crisp homemade page that was about three feet long with words and some images on the front and back. It was handwritten in ink—a mix of standard writing and glyphs, which were commonplace since the MegaCrash. The ink was very light. Nevel assumed politically-approved journalists made their own copies by creating an original in heavy ink before pressing it onto another page to copy before the ink had a chance to dry. It must have been a painstaking process, Nevel imagined. The paper had one large, leading story entitled "Building Our Defense."

"Check it out," Nevel said, pointing at the article. "It says 'The NADF is strong and only getting stronger. The force of Police and The Banded Brothers is unmatchable.' Wonder what NADF stands for? And what is The Banded Brothers?"

Quinn shrugged and continued leaning over his shoulder to read as Nevel held the paper. Intrigued,

Nevel read chunks quickly and silently while giving his opinions intermittently. "This whole paper is military. They must be really paranoid about attack."

"Think they've already been attacked?" Quinn asked.

"No, I think we would have seen evidence of that. But maybe they've seen things we haven't—enough to scare them."

Nevel read on. The main article was surrounded by advertisements calling to families to give up their men and boys to join The Banded Brothers. A sketch of a man with a mask and a rag of some kind tied around his arm gave Nevel a clue as to why the people in the streets had looked at his face and arm so strangely. He was an able boy and would have been expected to be a part of this volunteer militia.

"Guess I'm going to have to find a mask and a band if I am going to roam the streets here unquestioned," Nevel said.

"Yeah," Quinn said. "Now we know where all the men and boys have been. Check out this map. Their defense is huge. This isn't like Driscoll's crew of bandits. This is legit."

Quinn pointed at the map. The paper was clearly a platform to boast about the expanding military in the area that covered the Enoggera Army Barracks training center, which existed in the middle of Brisbane. It told of the activities at each location; drills, courses, and simulations were carried out here. In addition, the airport was listed on their map as part of the military defense.

"Look," Quinn said pointing at a part of the map

with drawings of airplanes. "There's one way to use your space after the MegaCrash." Nevel read in detail that what had formerly served as the Brisbane International Airport before the MegaCrash was now the CNADF, Center for the New Australian Defense Force. Nevel had read many Australian history books and knew that prior to the MegaCrash, Australia's Defense Force consisted of three branches; the Royal Australian Navy, the Australian Army, and the Royal Australian Air Force. With the crash of technology, clearly the airport now housed the CNADF and used what resources were available to create a new defense using history's examples.

"Look at this," Nevel said pointing at The Fort Lytton National Park, also shown on the map. "I've read about this place. It was a living museum before the MegaCrash. You know the type—where people dressed in old-timey clothing and reenacted battles and all." Nevel had set the paper in his lap and stretched his left arm out with his index finger extended and pulled his right hand in close to his chest with his thumb up and index finger curled as if holding a trigger while looking down the barrel of an invisible rifle. Quinn laughed.

"I used to really want to go to that place and be in a mock battle." Nevel laughed at himself and dropped his invisible rifle to pick the paper back up. "So now it's being used by the CNADF. It makes sense. The reenactments of battles used old cannons and powder guns. I'm sure that place taught them a lot about how to build a defense based on things that worked in a time before technology. Check this out." Nevel pointed out a small side article that was titled 'Brisbane's River City is a Magical Place to Live'.

"Ha!" Quinn laughed. "If you find depression, poverty, and disease magical!"

Nevel laughed too. It was clear the paper was a tool of the government used to brainwash the residents and keep them under their control.

"Well, we know a lot more now about how this place works," Nevel said. "Glad we got it."

"Agreed," Quinn said, looking away from the paper and around their new space, "We ought to clean this place up a bit—make use of what we can while we figure out what we will do."

"Agreed." Nevel grinned and they stood to take in their surroundings. It was a mess, Nevel knew that, but it was safer than anywhere they had been so far.

Together, they started clearing the room.

"This week you'll have to stay in. I'll go out alone, try to barter enough knowin' to get you some other clothes so you don't stand out. Even the old clothes we brought in the pack won't suit us here. I'll tie a band around my arm to fit in better, guess I'll need to tie a mask around my face too," Nevel said as he reassembled a cubicle back into a standing position. Quinn looked down at her pretty navy dress.

"I definitely stood out today—we both did—but I can't stay cooped up for too long so you better be quick with your trades." Quinn winked, but Nevel knew she was serious. She wasn't exactly the stay-at-home-wife type. She was already busy surviving, emptying a file cabinet of its paper contents now. "We can stack the papers here—they'll be great for burning- and I am pretty sure we can use one of these metal drawers for a fire pit. The other two I will use to try to grow some things so we can eat."

"Good idea," Nevel agreed, but he knew it would be tough to get soil up here. And he wondered how they would get water too. "We won't be able to light this place up at night—don't want anyone to see we are here. So I am going to put some desks and cubicles together and build us a sort of cave so we can have a little light at night underneath it." Nevel continued working to move cubicles and desks into a circle in the center of the room. Quinn continued stacking paper and emptying drawers and crates.

Quinn looked at the windows and put her hands on her hips. "We'll get plenty of light during the day so if you can get me some seeds I think I can make something grow. Some of the paper can be shredded to pot the plants, but I'll need a little dirt and water. We will only be able to survive off what we have in the pack for so long."

"I'll go out in a bit and see what I can do," Nevel said, "But I will have to move around, trade at different posts. Don't want people to be suspicious of me. It might take some time."

"I'm afraid all we've got right now is time," Quinn said with a smile and Nevel smiled back.

This was the last place he had seen her.

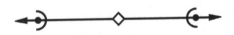

A bird's call snapped Nevel back into the moment. It was not a crow, only a gull.

Nevel paced back and forth along the shoreline. His palms were clammy and a lump began to grow in his throat. Where was she? Again, he cupped his hands over his eyes. This time he saw something.

A spot began to form on the horizon. Nevel rubbed his eyes and looked again. Yes, it was something! Only a few more moments and she began to come into view.

She was beautiful. His heart sank into the pit of his gut. Without even realizing he was speaking out loud, his whisper hopped on a wave and was carried out to sea to greet her. "She's a bute."

She was no redhead, but she was beautiful all the same. Her sails seemed to scrape the clouds. She was slowly, steadily, coming to port.

The lines of her iron hull were beautiful and sleek. Her lofty rigging made her appear light and graceful as she moved across the water. She was one of the few tall ships still in existence. Nevel had read about tall ships, great sailing vessels from a bygone age. A nineteenth century Square Rigger. Australia was proud to have her. She represented the development of Australia, as it was the tall ships, which brought goods to their shores as the country developed into a modern nation more than a century before. She had carried timber, wool, coal, and kerosene. She had been kept as a museum of sorts during the modern age, offering tours and glimpses into her historical past. Nowadays, Nevel knew the new Australian government must be happy to still have her, as she was one of few ships that could operate post-technology.

Nevel had learned in their time in the city that the government sent her to the islands close by to trade for fresh fruits and vegetables as well as spices. It was too risky to send her round Cape Horn where she surely had been dozens of times in her early days. She was kept close for now.

Now that he could finally confirm her arrival, Nevel ran from the sand back toward the broken asphalt that led to the city. He had to get to Quinn.

Nevel moved like he was being chased. He ran, legs launching him off the broken pavement and arms pumping, over bridges and canals through the river city. The tight muscles in his thighs allowed him to push off the ground with ease, catapulting him forward with each step. His arms swung back and forth, palms straight as arrows as he propelled himself towards the city. In the distance, Nevel could see the towers looming sharp against the sky. The high risers looked like silver daggers piercing the natural blue. Nevel's breaths were short and steady, his legs strong and swift. Miles in the outback had been much more difficult than this. The further he got from the beach and the closer he came to the city, the more the pit in his stomach grew. Life in the city had proven to be far different than the life Nevel had known in Morgan Creek. It had a darkness that hung over it even on the sunny days. With the veil lifted to expose a contemptible world of corruption and desperation, the city no longer did justice to the majestic pictures Nevel had seen of it in his books. Nevel felt claustrophobic here and he wanted out.

Just at the edge of the city now, Nevel pulled two

orange cloths from his pants pocket—one a mask he tied across his face, and the other a band he tied around his arm—before he moved through the city streets. These were requirements now, but the mask also repelled the stench and disease that filled the city. The smell became noticeable not far from the sands of the beaches. It was pungent and offensive, a combination of death and disease and waste piled high or burning. Nevel's feet carried him swiftly through the dirty city streets, packed with women, children, bartering posts over broken asphalt and cement, and the occasional loose chicken. A squish under his boot called his attention downward and he had to tuck his face into the corner of his elbow to breathe in and out and prevent himself from vomiting. His foot had plunged straight into a pile of feces that had been tossed in the street surely from a squat nearby.

Nevel scraped his boot along the sidewalk's edge and ran on amidst the noises of the traders. "You got a trade for knowin?" the peddler women called from their mid-street booths. Nevel slowed to a walk and put his hands in his pockets, even though he only held a stretch of rope and a few seeds. Shifty eyes darted in busy areas and pockets had to be guarded from theft. "Jewels here! Just a bit of knowin' will get you something real nice." Nevel weaved in and out of the crowded streets towards the government block. "Knowin'll getcha seeds here! Best ones around!" Shadows of the cityscape loomed from structures that now stood like the ancient pyramids—structures that could never be erected now without technology. Homemade flags made from ripped sheets whipped in the wind from the trading booths with their glyphs showing the kinds of information they were after: medical know-how, animal breeding, and more.

As the beggars and bartering posts became fewer and further between, he knew he was getting closer to his section of the city. Nevel finally reached the library to find a scene that took his breath away. Lines and lines of men and boys in black uniforms with orange bands around their right biceps and orange masks concealing their faces stood in formation. *Not today*, Nevel thought to himself.

Nevel had to get by the banded militia unseen or face joining them in drills. Sure, he looked like one of them as he ran through the streets, but that was to throw off the women and children. If he was seen by the men themselves, he would be forced to fall in line and join drills, something he avoided at all costs. He used a trick he had recently learned in the streets of this city. Ducking behind a corner, Nevel went to work. He took off his mask and band and tucked them away in his pocket. He then took off his shirt and draped it like a cape over his head, hiding his face. Next, he looked on the ground and searched for a bit of broken glass. In this city, broken glass seemed to be everywhere and so Nevel knew this would not be a daunting task. Spotting a bit of glass in a crack in the asphalt, he picked it up and took a deep breath before slicing a segment of his forearm until he saw thick crimson blood begin to seep out. He slashed himself quickly, but it stung nonetheless. He took his shirt and dabbed it in several places, letting the blood stain bright circles on his shirt on the outside. Once he had enough blood and was satisfied with the fresh stains it had made, he licked his wound and sucked on it a bit to stop the blood flow and replaced the now bloody cape to hide his face. Crouching and moving along the edges of the buildings leading to his alley, people would avoid him as he would clearly appear diseased. Still, Nevel's forehead beaded with sweat at the thought of a banded brother stopping him. Nevel moved swiftly past the crowds of militia and down the alleyway between his building and its high-rise neighbor full of baskets. Pulling his shirt back down and throwing it on unbuttoned so he could prepare to climb, he bumped into a dirty decrepit old beggar woman who was scraping a worm off of the asphalt. Her eyes shifted to Nevel with a carnal hunger that scared Nevel; he ran down the alley as fast as he could.

The rickety old fire escape hung ten feet above the ground. Nevel looked over his shoulder to make sure he wasn't being watched. He was alone. The beggar woman had vanished. A brick windowsill that jutted out about five feet up gave Nevel enough leverage to reach the black iron ladder and begin his climb up to Quinn. He moved quickly, skipping stairs as he went and pulling his weight up with both arms on the rails, so as only to be visible for seconds before leaping into the fifteenth floor window where he had left Quinn.

Once planted inside their flat, his knees almost gave way beneath him at what he found. Quinn was there, but not alone.

5

Fight

"Whatcha lookin at, bloke?" A seedy banded man at least ten years his senior looked up at Nevel with angry eyes from behind his orange mask. He had Quinn pinned against the floor with a broken bottle held tight to her neck. The man was stocky and short and was bleeding from beneath his mask; Quinn had obviously given him a fight. She had a bruise forming over her right eye, but no tears. Nevel knew the look she had in her eyes. She was no victim. Quinn was tough.

"Let the girl go," Nevel said as he stepped forward, trying to swallow the disgust welling in his throat.

"Don't take another step! You both are squatting

illegally. I'm taking you in!" the banded man challenged, but before he could finish his sentence, Quinn's knee lunged at his crotch and he rolled off of her just as Nevel jumped on him. Nevel's fist pounded his face. His knuckles slammed against bone and flesh through the cloth orange mask. Right hooks flew from Nevel in an uncontrollable rage. The man reached to swing at Nevel and Quinn sliced his arm with a piece of glass, tearing his sleeve to reveal a now bleeding tattoo of an iron fist over a book.

The man cried out, grabbing his bleeding arm and shuddering in pain. Nevel was back on him again, punching his face and stomach. Nevel knew the power the men of this city claimed to have merely because of the band on their arm, but he had seen them steal from children, make advances at women, and bypass the desperate needs of the sick and the elderly with cocky confidence. Quinn's attacker lay like a ragdoll on the cement floor, bleeding from behind the facemask and along his tattooed arm as Nevel continued pounding him in the stomach and face. Nevel was stronger than he had been a few months ago. He fought more like a man and less like a boy now. He was in an animal state, destroying this city vulture and protecting the girl. Punch after punch after punch, a rapid fire of hatred exploded on the victim. The banded brother tried a swing or two again, but was clearly out-powered.

Nevel was surprised at the emotion and power that came out of him as he defended Quinn. Finally Nevel felt arms on his shoulders tugging at him. He realized Quinn was trying to pull him off of the broken bloke.

"Easy, Nevel, you've made your point." She tried

to settle him down but his fists were still punching. Quinn caught his fist with her hand and looked him in the eye. He stopped and wiped his bloody lip on the back of his shirtsleeve, finally processing what was happening. His opponent was lying on the floor, half-conscious and moaning, holding his stomach and curled in a fetal position. He then passed out completely and fell limp on the floor.

"Bloody hell, Nevel, you almost killed 'em!" Quinn said.

"I just couldn't let him hurt you—" Nevel sputtered, still huffing and puffing from the brawl.

"He hadn't been here three minutes. I could have handled him," Quinn said, wiping her brow with her sleeve.

"Where did he come from?" Nevel's eyes were darting around the room as if to look for more adversaries.

"I was looking out the window for you. He was on the street. Taking a break from drills, I guess." Quinn took Nevel's chin in her fingertips and turned his head to look her in the eyes. "He saw me and I guess he came up the same way we do. He was alone. He said he was going to turn me in for squatting up here unknown. I wasn't going anywhere with him…"

Quinn was sitting next to him on the floor on the pile of junk where the fight had landed them. She blotted his wounded lip with her rag.

"It's awful here," she said with her back to her passed-out assailant.

"I'm tossing him out," Nevel said, leaning back from her blotting dismissively as he looked flippantly toward the hall where they never went and then looked to the window in deep thought.

"You can't just throw him out the window," Quinn replied.

"I know. I'm gonna take him down a few flights of stairs and let someone else deal with him when he wakes." Nevel scooped the man under his armpits and began to drag him. He was thick and heavy; one look at the aged hands that dragged limply behind the unconscious body told Nevel that the man was probably older than he had originally realized. "Are you going to take off his mask and look at his face?" Quinn asked with a wince.

"No need," Nevel said. "They're all the same."

Nevel dragged him to the interior of the building where the stairs were. The man was heavy and Nevel strained to drag him, but the adrenaline still rushing through his veins gave him enough strength to get him to the stairs.

"And when he wakes up? What then? He'll turn us in." Quinn was pacing now as she followed Nevel to the stairs where they had never before dared roam.

"When he wakes up, we'll be gone." Nevel huffed as he dragged the man out backwards and disappeared down the stairway.

"Where are you going to leave him?" Quinn called after him, but he was already gone.

Nevel knew this man was too heavy to drag up any flights of stairs, so he dragged the banded assailant down the stairs, his body thumping on each step. Nevel's grip under his armpits left the assailant's feet and legs lifelessly sliding as Nevel moved. After counting four flights, Nevel dropped the still masked and passed out assailant in the empty stairwell before returning quickly back to Quinn to escape being spotted.

Back in the cement room they had called home for months, Quinn was standing at the window in her patchwork pants and thin white shirt biting her nails nervously. She was not close enough to the window that anyone on the street could spot her now. Nevel stood and watched her, taking her in. Too many times he had come close to losing her. He had lost control in the fight. His love for her rivaled the violence he showed to protect her. Nevel took a long, deep breath in to settle the testosterone that still rushed through his veins. He brushed his sweaty hands along his patchwork pants and smeared his forehead with the sleeve of his shirt. They were both thinner and paler than they had been when they arrived. He walked to the window to join her, putting his left palm on the flat of her back, and looked out at the depressing sight. "Yeah, it ain't exactly the outback. We'll be out of here soon enough, though."

"Where are we gonna go?" Quinn tossed her hands in surrender, "We can't stay here now. As soon as that guy wakes up, he'll lead a pile of men up here to us. We've got nowhere else to go. It isn't like we can just move in with the neighbors!"

He stopped and turned to her. "The ship's here."

"It's here?" Quinn squealed as she wrapped her arms around Nevel. "Finally! I thought it would never come!"

She let go and looked at Nevel with the same look

she had given him when they dropped from the rock and when they boarded the train. It was a look that had adventure written all over it.

6

Inventory

"The plan," Nevel started, "is to be in line first thing in the morning for crew like we discussed."

They had discussed it—over and over again—in the weeks that they had waited, trying to stay alive and hidden in a city where they were sitting ducks.

They sipped from the same soup they had been living on all week. It was brothy, full of herbs Quinn had grown in her file-cabinet drawer garden. Looking at the floor they sat on, both were quiet. Nevel was deep in thought.

"We need to go through our stuff and get our plan straight one last time before we head to port," Nevel announced, taking charge of the operation. So much had happened. So much had changed in such a small amount of time. Their very identities had evolved and were about to change again.

"And the banded bloke?" Quinn asked turning to Nevel. "Reckon' he's out for the night?"

"Yeah, he won't wake until we're gone. I made sure he was breathing, but he's out."

Nevel opened their pack, pulling out items and naming them as if taking inventory for a store. Some were items they had brought with them in their pack from Morgan Creek. Some were acquired since their time in the city. They had been careful to keep them, recognizing their value. What little food that had originally been in the pack that his father prepared for him was long gone by now.

"Blanket...flint and steel...Pass of the Crow...rope...knife," He stopped at the knife and they both shared a smile, knowing it had once almost taken his life. Nevel resumed the inventory, "...your *Pride and Prejudice*...the Register."

At the word, Nevel stopped and looked to Quinn. They had discussed the Register at length since they had lived in the city. Quinn and Nevel didn't really understand it, but they knew it was important...so important they could be killed for it. They had read it dozens of time during their squat in the city; each reading yielded the same results—nothing.

"You know, you can still change your mind; you can still leave without me..." Quinn spoke softly as she turned and faced the empty room.

"And why would I do that?" Nevel said, grabbing her left arm softly and turning her back to him.

"Because it's just going to be harder with me. I

47

know we have discussed a plan, but I also know I'm more of a risk than an asset. You have an important job to do for the UBM—for the whole bloody world! I could mess that up! Is that really worth it? You don't have to be stuck with me is all. I'm tough." Quinn stared at Nevel with a seriousness he hadn't seen since the jail back home. He took her hands in his, but it didn't break her steady tone as she continued. "I'd be OK if you needed to go on without me."

"I could never..." Nevel started, rising to his feet as Quinn followed suit.

"Yes. Yes, you could." Quinn let go of Nevel's hands and started pacing the room while Nevel stood stunned. "I don't want to be the reason you fail." Nevel was dumfounded as he listened to her. They had discussed the plan. They had confirmed that they were in this together. Quinn continued pacing and talking, never meeting Nevel's eyes. "You have an obligation to the UBM." Nevel tried to move to make eye contact as she rambled on, but she stayed a step ahead. "I'm just a girl—"

Nevel finally stepped in the line of her pacing and stopped her in her tracks. He pulled her chin up with his index finger, forcing her to look at him instead of the floor. "Quinn, you have never been 'just a girl.' You are the reason I am free to be me now."

Quinn held his stare for a moment and then dropped her eyes again to the floor. "I forced you out. I already almost had you killed several times now! What if that banded bloke had caught you off guard and stabbed you before you could even fight..." Quinn said to Nevel who threw his hands up in surrender before speaking his mind.

"My whole life I've hidden, I've lived a lie. I have watched from the shadows while others lived. I told my parents that night at my house in front of you—I'm done with the hiding and the sitting around and hoping I never get noticed; it's no way to live! And I would have eventually come to that realization even if you had never come along." His palms were sweating. He stood again and walked toward the window. He brushed his hair back out of his face and took a deep breath before continuing. Some things he just had to say, no matter how difficult. He turned back toward her. She was looking at him now. Her green eyes were on his, not the floor. Her long, red hair was brushed off her shoulders and her lips were open. He spoke honestly from his heart. "Something about you makes me more scared than I have ever felt, but at the exact same time makes me more brave than I have ever been. You make me feel like I can do anything. I won't succeed without you." Nevel's voice became a bit shaky and he swallowed to clear the lump that was forming as he looked at the girl he loved. Unbidden, his mind spun to a page in *Great Expectations*: '*Love her, love her, love her! If she favours you, love her. If she wounds you, love her. If she tears your heart to pieces—and as it gets older and stronger, it will tear deeper—love her, love her, love her!*' But it was easier for Dickens to write than for him to say. He couldn't tell her he loved her. Not yet.

He swallowed again the lump that continued to try to creep up his throat and looked her dead in her green eyes and forced her to believe him. "I will never leave you. I will always come back to you. Over and over again, it will still be you. Only you."

Quinn blushed and she blinked abundantly to try to keep her calm.

"OK, OK," she said through a cracking voice, seemingly embarrassed.

"I'm all in," Nevel said, still forcing her to lock eyes.

"Me too," Quinn whispered, as if those two simple words used siphoned the only bit of breath she had left.

Nevel stepped closer to Quinn, so close their breaths bounced off of each other. Nevel's lips weren't an inch from Quinn's. His heart pounded in his chest. He wanted to kiss her. They hadn't shared a kiss since the tunnel; maybe he had been too busy focusing on surviving the city or perhaps his nerves had taken hold. If ever there was a time to kiss her, he knew it was now. He looked straight into her green eyes and felt butterflies teem and swirl in his stomach. His mind filled with poetry: Shakespearean Sonnets, Sonnets from the Portuguese, e.e. cummings. She closed her eyes. He leaned in. Their lips met and electric currents coursed through his veins. His hands pulled her head closer. She wrapped her arms around him and the kiss released and turned into a tight hug.

"Penny for your thoughts," Nevel said with a grin, making a new joke from an old saying, as he pulled away from their hug to look at Quinn's face.

"Well, you must not care much about what I'm thinking with a worthless offer like that!" Quinn said with a smirk and Nevel laughed as she continued,

"And I'm sure all the while you're just reading a novel in that head of yours!"

Nevel was glad to have broken the seriousness as he picked her up and lifted her high above him, spinning wildly as she spread her arms like a bird, a crow even. "We stay together!" Nevel chanted and Quinn laughed. He set her, giggling, back onto her feet and looked at her with gratitude. He still couldn't believe she was there with him. Nevel tried to refocus.

"Let's look at the Register again, just in case, maybe we're missing something-"

"Of course," Quinn said sarcastically, "we've hardly given it a glance."

Nevel knew she was poking fun at him. They had read it hundreds of times and had not yet figured it out. He knew she wondered why now would be any different.

Grabbing the Register from the pack where they kept it, Nevel sat inside their cubicle tower in the center of the room with Quinn. He read aloud the same lists and locations of books they had read so many times until he reached the end. Nevel focused on the locations as he scanned up and down the pages. Sydney, Brisbane, Alice Springs—nothing surprising, still when he began to come across locations like New Zealand, Fiji, Venice, Paris, Bangkok— he still couldn't believe the books had traveled that far. These books had been to places he didn't even know still existed since the MegaCrash. More importantly, the U.B.M truly was a worldwide organization and this was proof. And he was a part of it.

"That's it?" Quinn asked.

"That's it," Nevel affirmed, still mystified.

It was getting dark. Nevel left the Register open to the last page in his lap and struck the flint and steel.

"WAIT!!" Quinn screamed, jumping from her seat on the cement floor. "There's more!!"

Nevel looked at Quinn like she was crazy. "What are you doing?!" Nevel asked Quinn who had launched herself into his lap where the book sat.

"I saw a clue!" Quinn retorted emphatically.

Nevel held the book up and looked at Quinn in confusion.

"I read it all, Quinn," he insisted. "We've read it a thousand times."

"When you struck the flint and steel, when the light was reflecting on the book, there was something I saw, on the last page. It looked blank, but it showed up when you lit it up."

Nevel furrowed his brow in confusion, but again struck the flint and steel, this time lighting one of their premade paper torches. Quinn held the book up to the blank last page by his light. Letters began to glow from a space that had seemingly been void of writing seconds before.

"You're right!" Nevel shouted in disbelief, his eyes wide on the page and his fingers running across the invisible ink.

7

Clue

Against the light, the thin, seemingly blank page had a message written on it. Nevel assumed it was some kind of oil as he let his fingers run across it again and again. It had no color or texture, but the words Nevel read aloud were clear.

"*Let us exhume the culture of our past.*" Nevel said each word slowly and carefully and then repeated them again, "Let us exhume the culture of our past."

"What does it mean?" Quinn asked Nevel. "Do you think your dad wrote that for us? Why didn't he just tell us?" Quinn was confused, and so was Nevel. The Register lay in her lap. They both intermittently looked down at it and then out into the room, deep in thought.

"I don't know. If it's a line from literature, I don't remember reading it in my library. I don't know who wrote it. I mean, maybe it was not from literature at all. Maybe U.B.M..." Nevel stood and started pacing, still holding the torch with one hand and scratching his head with the other.

"You better put that out," Quinn said looking up at the torch that Nevel was unknowingly parading through the room as he became lost in his train of thought. He didn't seem to even realize she had spoken as he continued pacing and rambling on, torch in hand.

Quinn jumped up and took the torch from him, dropping it in the tin can holder on the floor in the cavern of desks where they sat at night to block the light.

"I know there are people above my dad. Maybe it's from them?" Nevel walked back and squatted next to Quinn where she now sat holding the book in the hollow of a desk, huddling by the hidden tin can of firelight. Together they used the tin can light to scour the page, searching for more. They still saw only what Nevel had read aloud. "Maybe my dad doesn't even know about this message. Good eye, though, Quinn. I would never have seen it. We may not have ever known about this." Nevel seemed a bit disappointed in himself at the thought of almost missing this clue. He stood again and paced.

"We're better together, Nevel," Quinn reminded him as he stood at the dark window looking out.

"Agreed," he said and turned from the window. He came back to her and sat. They dropped the topic of the Register again; it was a topic they had exhausted time and time again. Now they refocused on what would happen the next day.

"You know, you're gonna have to cut my hair," Quinn said, handing Nevel a long blade of glass that reflected the moonlight. They had saved it for this very moment. By now it was sharper than the blade of their knife despite the number of times they sharpened it. When they had found this particular blade of glass, they knew it would make for the least painful of haircuts and so they set it aside until the time came. Nevel took it in his hand and she turned her back to him and released her long, beautiful locks from the knot tied atop her head.

"Quinn, I'm really sorry, I…"

"Just do it, already," Quinn said. "The more you talk about it the more I think about it. It's hair; it'll grow back. I gotta look the part."

Nevel knew she was right. It had been part of the plan. They had discussed this would be a necessary evil. Nevel took the glass in his right hand and took a fist of red hair in his left.

"Ready?"

"Ready."

He cut her thick red strands in jagged pieces. At first Nevel tried cutting too much hair at once, making it difficult to cut through the stands that were thicker. He quickly learned to take smaller chunks at a time to make the process easier. Nevel held small fistfuls of hair in sections, pulling out from her scalp, and cut. Quinn didn't say a word.

"I'm not hurting you, am I?" Nevel often checked,

to which Quinn would only answer by shaking her head no. She was silent. He worried what it meant. He continued to cut. He turned to hand her a fist full of red locks. He swore her eyes were glossy with tears, but he knew she would never admit it. They had decided not to trade the hair at market, though it could have bought them a chicken. A chicken couldn't travel with them. They could have cut her hair earlier, but they decided they only would if they ran out of food before the ship arrived.

"It's just hair," Quinn said again quietly, sitting in a pile of soft, red falling snow. At the last drop of red, she blew out the torch. "We better get some sleep. Tomorrow we're sailors."

8

Test

Before climbing out the window for the last time, Nevel looked back over his shoulder to the room they had called home in this dirty city. They left their squat cleaner than they had found it. It looked like a museum of the technology era: desks sat with silent phones and still computer monitors, items Quinn and Nevel had cleaned and left undisturbed because there was nothing else to do with them. Nevel didn't feel sad at all leaving this place. It had served its purpose as their hideout for the weeks they had been here, but it was no home. There was no family cooking in the kitchen, no photos hanging on the walls, no dog waiting on the porch. Nevel swallowed a lump and shook it off. It was time to move on again.

They walked through the government block and into the crowded, dreadful city streets. Today Nevel wasn't as worried about being in plain sight as a man who could be recruited into the Banded Brothers. Today he was worried about Quinn, who now appeared to be a boy just like him. She wore a t-shirt over her bandaged chest; though she didn't have much to give her away as a female in that sense, they couldn't take any chances. Nevel had blushed at the conversation when she brought it up. They agreed to claim that she (he) had been stabbed in the side and hence the wrapping around the chest. She wore a pair of slacks that they had traded for weeks before. The slacks were dirty and baggy and covered her pretty, long legs.

Ducking in and out of alleys as they made their way to the port, Nevel prayed they would remain unnoticed. As they walked, they didn't talk much. They were playing new roles and both were reviewing them in their heads. Quinn had the more difficult role to play and Nevel worried about her ability to pull it off. Their walk was a long one. They had only taken this walk once before to be sure of the location, but they hadn't dared go again as the port was riddled with police and Banded Brothers protecting their land from seafaring attackers.

The dismal cityscape changed slowly as they drew nearer to the port. The skyscrapers grew shorter and more spread apart. The street even grew wider. It was as if the city made way for the majestic sea.

Finally the city stench yielded to saltier, fresher air carried by sea winds and the city buildings had all but disappeared. In the distance, Nevel could see the water between the lines of police and Banded Brothers standing guard. The water was flanked by docks and smaller boats and warehouses. The smell of fish pervaded, but it was a welcome change to the city's stench of human demise. Gulls cried and new sounds of splashing and creaking docks and stretching lines of rope filled Nevel's ears. He was excited.

His eyes fell on the lines of would-be sailors, glad to see he and Quinn were not the first—so as not to appear too eager—nor the last, as he looked over his shoulder and saw many men in the distance walking this way. Here, lines of men who, like them, had opted out of the banded brotherhood stood and waited for a chance at adventure on the seas. The danger at sea was much greater at this point than that of the army as no war had yet come to fruition. Many hoped they would gain hero status without ever having to commit to anything but the drills they did safely within their barracks. This was why the lines at port were nowhere near the length of the lines of Banded Brothers who marched through the dirty city streets.

Quinn and Nevel chose different lines to reduce any suspicion.

"Next!" A voice boomed and seemed to bounce off of the blue sky and straight into the blue sea below.

Nevel stepped his booted foot onto a rusty silver scale. He stared blankly straight ahead while a small, gray-haired man with bifocals took a tape and wrapped it around his waist and chest and arms. As the tailor scribbled on his ledger, Nevel took in his surroundings. In front of him stood half a dozen burly

59

men in stained t-shirts and ragged pants. Their biceps were bulging and stamped with tattoos of anchors and nautical flags boasting seafaring careers. Nevel glanced at his own biceps, free of ink and smaller than those of several of the men around him, but far bigger now than they were before his adventures with Quinn. His cheeks flushed red for a fleeting moment as he was embarrassed to be under physical scrutiny, but he quickly took a deep breath and regained composure. Another man was now looking in his eyes and throat with a medical instrument. It had been so long since Nevel had had a check-up of any kind. He had always been a healthy child. He worried the city would have made him sick and so he and Quinn had avoided time in the city streets as much as possible. As the man moved to listen to Nevel's heart, Nevel looked left.

A few rows to his left at this Port of Call B, Quinn stood in line, also staring straight ahead. The dirty pants and the oversized t-shirt made her look like a boy—that and the fact that her hair was cut short and tucked under her hat, jagged pieces of red uneven behind her ears. She was still beautiful to Nevel, even more so now that he had seen her unyielding courage to cut the hair she so clearly cherished but insisted would grow back anyway. Girls didn't sail in crew. It would have to be their little secret.

"Move along," a bearded officer barked at the lines as they marched through weigh-ins, physicals, competency tests, and crew assignments. Nevel frequently glanced at Quinn inconspicuously to check on her. She stuck out like a sore thumb in this crowd, younger and smaller than the others, but so did he.

Like him, she had now passed through the weigh-in as well as the physical check of her eyesight, vitals, and hearing. Luckily, it wasn't their size that they would depend upon to get them on this ship.

Nevel stepped forward again with the rhythm of his line and watched as Quinn neared the competency section of her line and stood face to face with the skipper. Nevel strained to listen in as he watched a conversation take place, but the muttering of sailors waiting in line mixed with the chattering of seagulls, wind gusts, and the splashing of water against the moorings disallowed his eavesdropping.

His palms became wet and his heartbeat grew rapid. Nevel hoped they had prepared enough. He watched as she appeared to answer question after question until she was pointed in a new direction. Nevel swallowed, looking at Quinn for a reaction. Was she turned away? Was her voice giving her away? So many young boys still had high pitched-voices. He hoped her youth would excuse it. Her back was to him and he could not decide if she had passed or failed. He craned his neck to see around the men that stood in lines between them. She was blocked from his view. It was evident the ship would have brawn based on their competitors in line, but he knew crew members with brain power were just as valuable on these sailing vessels as captains navigated treacherous waters without modern technology. Nevel stepped forward again, dangerously close to the sailor in front of him and he tried not to breathe heavily on his neck as he leaned in to try to see Quinn. Suddenly, Quinn was again in his sight. She looked at him with a stoic face, but a twinkle in her green eyes. In her hand she held a uniform. She had passed! Nevel's elation was cut short as his line pushed him forward and he approached the skipper.

"Point starboard." Nevel pointed right. He couldn't believe she had made it. Soon, they would be at sea. Nevel had never been on a boat in his life. He had only read about them in the books in his mind. He did not know how to swim, which scared him a bit, but he craved the chance to learn. He imagined the feeling of being immersed in the blue water, defying gravity; underwater must be as close as one could get to the feeling of flying.

"Leaving harbor, green buoys must be kept to which side?" the skipper continued his quiz. The competency section was difficult for many in this day and age; Nevel knew they had an advantage due to the library in his head. Most sailors who were accepted came from a long line of mariners and gained their knowledge first hand over their lifetime from grandfathers and uncles and dads teaching them all that there was to know of ships and the sea.

"Starboard, sir." Nevel smiled at the thought of their new adventure upon this trade ship heading towards Papua New Guinea, the Philippines, and Asia. He scanned titles of books in his mind's library on the animals and customs of these countries and was overjoyed at the thought of all that they would experience.

"What is the halyard?" the skipper asked as he scribbled on his ledger.

"A line used for raising or lowering sails, sir." The answers came easily to Nevel. He had them all stored in the library in his mind. It was Quinn who had had to cram for this exam, but she had always been a good student. Now that she had passed, their plan was taking form.

"What is the maneuver when the boat is made to change direction by passing the stern of the boat through the wind?"

"Jibe." Nevel continued his Q and A with the skipper, waiting for its end so he too could claim his uniform and then rejoin Quinn.

"What's that?" the skipper asked to a uniformed officer to his right.

"OK, crew's full. Better luck next time," the skipper dismissed Nevel.

"What? What do you mean?" Nevel paced in a panic, looking around him as the lines began to clear and disappointed faces headed back toward the city. His forehead beaded in sweat. His heartbeat raced.

"No, I have to be on this ship," Nevel pleaded to the skipper who was already walking away.

"Ship's full," was all the skipper said.

9
Uniform

Nevel met Quinn's confused gaze from across the shipyard as she was prodded toward the ship with a crew of strangers.

Nevel looked to his feet and then to the sky. What more could he offer without giving himself away?

"I speak Filipino!" Nevel shouted.

"What's that?" The skipper stopped and turned around, looking at Nevel incredulously.

"I speak Filipino." Nevel was quieter this time, desperately trying to think of an explanation as he pulled his Filipino translation dictionary from the library in his mind.

The skipper waved at the uniformed officer who had called off the search for additional crew moments before. The man was thin and tall with a coarse salt and pepper black mustache. Nevel stood still, watching, as the uniformed officer with the grey and black mustache came back to where the skipper was, eyes rolling at the inconvenience of being called back. It appeared the skipper was filling him in. Meanwhile, Nevel prepared himself for what would surely come next.

"How the bloody hell does an Aussie like you know Filipino?" the mustached officer demanded as he approached.

"My great uncle used to be in the navy. He married a Filipino, my great aunt. She taught me before she died," Nevel lied through his teeth as he turned to a page in the translation dictionary in his mind.

"Kamusta kamusta ka," Nevel continued, now speaking in Filipino to prove his worth. "It means *hello, how are you.*" The officer was inches from Nevel's face, snarling at him as he took him in.

"Anyone can learn hello!" The officer laughed and took two steps back. "I want to hear something more. Show me you can bargain for us when we trade." He crossed his arms across his chest and cocked his head as he waited for Nevel to accept his challenge.

Nevel took a step forward, crossing his own arms across his chest, and spoke fluently and eloquently, staring straight into the officer's eyes.

"Hindi kami tumatanggap ng ito kalakalan. Ito ay hindi patas. Nag-aalok kami sa iyo kalakal ng mahusay na halaga. Ano ang maaari mong nag-aalok sa mga bumabalik?"

"What does it mean?" the stunned officer asked.

"We do not accept this trade. It is not fair. We offer you goods of great value. What can you offer in return?" Nevel said.

The officer exploded in a bellowing laugh and looked to the skipper in disbelief.

"Well, it seems we've got room for one more on board," the officer grinned greedily. "Get this one a uniform."

Nevel felt an overwhelming sense of relief. Today his photographic memory was a blessing instead of a curse. With uniform in hand, he ran to catch up with the rest of the crew.

"Q," Nevel called as the line of men boarded the clipper, "wait up."

Nevel was weaving around the line trying to get to her. Quinn walked on, trying to continue to blend in.

"Hey brother," she replied gruffly with her chin tucked as he finally caught up to her. The sailors around them didn't seem interested, but this was the plan they had created in the days leading up to the arrival of the ship; they were to be brothers. Nevel was relieved to fall in line behind her as they approached the dock.

"You had me a little worried," Quinn whispered under her breath.

"Yeah, me too," Nevel replied as they walked on with chins tucked to their chests as they continued their whispered conversation.

"What happened?" Quinn asked.

"I almost didn't get on. They said the ship was full just as I was about to pass."

"So how'd you manage?" Quinn looked at him briefly, still hushed.

"Had to pull out a few tricks." Nevel winked.

His arrogance was quickly replaced by humility as he walked from dirt road onto dock and could see the water between the planks splashing unpredictably beneath him. Sweat pooled beneath the folds in his arms and dripped down his face. In his mind, he was scanning books on water safety and trying to learn to swim by looking at the pictures of the strokes. He doubted it would help, but he felt he had to do something.

The ship awaited her crew at the end of the dock. The line marched forward and the closer the men came to the ship, the quieter they got. All eyes were on her.

Up close now, Nevel forgot about his fear of drowning and basked in the majestic creation that she was. Her iron hull was painted black with a golden line of trim. A scrollwork ornamentation decorated her bow. Her more than twenty sails whipped in the wind above like flags of victory over a modern age, which now surrendered again to the days of old. The masthead stretched easily one hundred feet above deck.

A long plank flanked by rope banisters led up to the port stern of the ship. Already on board was a captain standing on the port bow watching his crew arrive. He was older with a gray beard and gray curled locks spilling from his hat. His uniform was starched white with navy and gold stripes and brass buttons. He looked like the naval officers in the books in Nevel's mind. His white hat was flat and pressed, the navy bill clean and the anchor embellishment shining in gold cord. Even from a distance, Nevel could see the aura of respect this man commanded on his ship. He looked tall and fit as he stood watch over his crew.

Stepping over lines from stern towards bow, the new crew approached the center of the ship and stopped at the first mate's hand signal.

"Men, I introduce you to your Captain. Captain William Way."

The men cheered. Nevel and Quinn clapped and stared, not knowing what to expect.

The captain took three steps forward to a place on the bow that overlooked the crew. The cheers continued until he held his hand out in command to silence them. Then the captain began to speak. "Welcome to the Lilian Ruth," his booming voice echoed. "I owe her my life, and so will you." The raucous crew stood taller and seemed to straighten themselves up a bit. All listened with intensity. All eyes were on the captain. "She will be the one reason we live or die at sea. Treat her as the queen that she is. Follow orders. That is all. Fall out and let us get underway!"

Again the crew cheered. The captain walked away and was joined by higher-level officers. The crew fell back into a line that led back toward the center of the ship. The line fed into an opening where sailors began funneling below one by one. Below deck, crates and bunks were stacked so close together, Nevel wondered how they would breathe. The space was smaller and more confined than the inside of the depository he and Quinn had discovered in the outback. The air was warm and moist and smelled of body odor as the sixteen crewmembers, including Nevel and Quinn, dropped their bags on bunks arranged in twin lines, a row on either side of the vessel. Nevel made sure he chose a bunk below Quinn. She would be safer up high, away from grabbing hands. A chattering amongst the sailors filled the chamber and echoed off the walls, making it difficult for Nevel to hear as Quinn tried to say something.

"What's that?" he asked, but she responded with furrowed brows as if she too was confused and couldn't make out what he was saying. He shrugged at her and they both continued about their bunks, getting settled in like everyone else. Nevel dropped his pack on his bunk and immediately worried about the safety of its contents. He was following protocol. This was what the UBM had wanted: *take the R to sea, port of call B.*

He ran his hands through the bag, but didn't dare remove anything. Nevel could feel the ship moving atop the slippery sea. He felt queasy. It was hot below deck and the smell of these unkempt men was stifling. Looking around, it was clear that this was the time to get into uniform. All men were ripping shirts and pants off and replacing them with the uniforms that were white with navy stitching along the edges. The men were tying bandanas made of the same white cloth with navy etching around their heads and slipping on shoes with sturdy rubber soles.

Nevel swallowed nervously and looked to Quinn who was sitting on her top bunk. She pulled her shirt off, exposing the wrapping only for a split-second, and immediately replaced it with her new uniform.

Nevel scanned the crowd for nosy on-lookers. These men were not interested in this young boy's injury. They had even been careful enough to dab blood on the outside of the bandage on one side to make it appear she was in fact bleeding from a wound. Nevel breathed a sigh of relief as Quinn was now covered and he shed his clothes to replace them with his new uniform.

"Starboard watch there, Port watch there," a crew member who was about Nevel's height, but with a husky, stout build and a bald head said to Nevel as he pointed right and then left at the bunks.

"Right, thanks." Nevel ducked as a burly man tossed his sack right over Nevel's head and onto the top bunk next to Quinn's. Quinn, now in uniform complete with a bandana wrapped around her newly jagged red locks, was sitting unnoticed on her bunk looking at her new surroundings. Nevel stood and watched the bald sailor take the low bunk next to him.

"No water comes in here. Cap'n' s fine," he said and then coughed and spit a hunk of something on the floor. "Gotta watch out for the first mate. Don't let 'em catcha idle. Everything 'round here's gotta stay shipshape. First voyage, eh?" The bald sailor's kind voice was in stark contrast to his bulbous body. He smiled at Nevel and his teeth were gray and crooked. He smelled of sweat and whisky.

"How'd you know?" Nevel asked, trying to make light of the fact that he clearly was no sailor.

"Name's David." The bald sailor reached out his tattooed arm to shake Nevel's hand. The tattoo was a seagull with a fish in its mouth.

"Nevel." Nevel offered his hand and grimaced at the tight squeeze it was given within the calloused, huge hands of the sailor. They had decided to use their real names. It wouldn't matter now that they were so far from Morgan Creek. Quinn would be short for Quincy if he accidentally called her Quinn instead of Q.

On her bunk, Quinn peeked down but quickly looked right back onto her bunk, folding the dirty t-shirt and slacks and storing them at the head of her bed for a pillow.

"All hands on deck!" Orders were being barked from above.

Immediately, all sailors began filing up the ladder and through the tiny opening in the center of their dwelling. Quinn dropped down from her bunk and lined up in front of Nevel, but not before offering him a glance as if to say, *we can do this*. It was exactly what Nevel needed to summon the courage to climb to the deck and begin his stint as a sailor.

10
Underway

The crew fell in line as long lengths of rope were placed in their hands. Hand over fist, Nevel and Quinn pulled at the sheets while white cloaks straightened up the mast. The whipping wind was popping in choppy bursts through the rising white sails, sounding like a barking dog. Soon, the sail filled entirely with wind, and the choppy, bumpy clambering across the channel suddenly turned into a swiftly smooth ride. They were underway.

For the entirety of the day, all hands were on deck. When they were not pulling at the lines attached to the sails, they were bailing the water that crept in with the crash of waves over the bow. The shifts, they were told, would begin tonight with starboard watch.

Nevel was glad to be on port watch. He was tired and he knew Quinn was too. His hands were rubbed raw from the ropes and his biceps felt like they would catch fire. He worried about Quinn. She managed to get herself on bailing duty more often than at the ropes and Nevel was glad of it; it was the job that required less strength. She was agile on the boat and was proving her worth with the bailing buckets. Nevel, on the other hand, slipped more than once when a wave crashed over the bow. He was glad to have the sheet line to hold, even if his palms were now pink and sore.

A constant wind kept the ship moving, but busy. Nevel was delighted to see dolphins swim up by the boat, ducking in and out of the water playfully as if to challenge the boat to mimic their movement.

"Didn't use to see 'em back in the day," David called over his shoulder to Nevel as they tugged at the sheet line.

"Why not?" Nevel asked.

"Humans had about killed 'em off. Since the MegaCrash the sea's come back 'ta life!" Nevel met Quinn's glance from across the deck. He pointed to the dolphins with a tilt of his head and she looked out at them and grinned wildly before looking back at Nevel with wide eyes that were full of tentative hope. He knew what she was thinking; it couldn't have been far off from what he was thinking: *this is amazing.*

The sun began to dip on the horizon and the wind settled a bit. The ship sailed swiftly across light swells now of about three feet. The yellow sun turned orange and the sky grew pink. With the sky, so went the color of the water—a mirror reflecting so well that Nevel wondered whether the birds would ever get so lost in flight that they might forget which was the sea and which was the sky. All the while, Quinn continued bailing what little water washed over now and Nevel pulled at sheets as officers commanded. Soon a blanket of darkness began to stretch out and cover the sea as the sky danced with thousands of tiny flickering stars.

"Starboard watch!" the first mate called and Quinn, Nevel, David and three other men ceased their work as they were replaced and headed down to the cabin below.

That first night on the ship Nevel was so tired and scorched by the sun, he craved the chance to sleep. Below deck, he and Quinn both laid down without a blanket or even taking off the shoes they had been grateful to have been given as part of their uniform and fell into a deep slumber.

Nevel was awoken in what seemed to be the middle of the night by a harmonica. Several of the crew were drinking, singing, and telling stories. Nevel tried sleeping through it. One man's voice carried something familiar. Nevel felt he was half-dreaming. The men were laughing and raucous, talking about a shark that had circled their boat on another voyage and one man boasting about pulling a knife and claiming, "He can't kill me, not if I kill him first!"

Nevel sat up in bed. In the dark, no one noticed his sudden action. No one could make out the sweat beading on his brow. The words had jarred him out of his half-slumber. *Not if I kill him first.* Nevel peered out at the men from his bunk. In the dark, they were oblivious to Nevel. *Not if I kill him first* rang again and again in Nevel's head. He had heard that before, in the depository. The man who wanted the Register had said it about Nevel's father. It was just a coincidence, Nevel reassured himself, lying back down and gripping his pack tightly in his arms. He finally fell back asleep.

A gong sounded. Its tone reverberated through their small chamber and filled Nevel's ears and head. Nevel and Quinn were called to wake for their next shift with the others. They awoke already dressed but checked their uniforms, half-asleep, as the ship wobbled and caused them to bump into each other. A short black-haired, stocky man with a new government tattoo on his arm of an iron fist over a book caught Nevel's eye. There was a cut along his tattoo that was scabbed. Nevel swallowed. He had a black eye and a split lip too. It couldn't be, Nevel thought to himself, plenty of the sailors on this ship looked just as beat up. Sailors were known for their disorderly behavior. Nevel dismissed the coincidence and continued to dress. The man seemed to notice Nevel's stare and returned it, asking with a chuckle, "Sleep well?"

"Yeah, yeah, you?" Nevel replied groggily as he tried to remain nonchalant.

"Crow kept me up," the man replied and looked straight into Nevel's eyes.

"Ha! Ain't no damn crows at sea, ya fool!" David laughed as he tied his hair back with his bandana.

Nevel's eyes shifted to Quinn and then the man again, not knowing what to think.

Ignore it, Quinn's eyes seemed to say, so they stood at attention waiting for orders.

The first mate began to roll call. "Anderson, Arden, Atchisy, "

"Aye" each sailor replied as his name was called.

"Branson," the first mate called. The hairs on the back of Nevel's neck stood up.

"Aye," said the man not five feet up from Nevel with a tattoo on his arm of the new government flag of an iron fist over a book interrupted by a fresh wound across it.

It couldn't be, Nevel thought to himself. The words rang in Nevel's mind again. *Not if I kill him first*! Then Nevel remembered the man's name he had overheard in the cave at the depository. Branson.

11

Storm

The wind vane was whipping back and forth at the top of the main mast. A booby bird continually tried to perch on it and was throwing off the navigation. Quinn was sent up as a scarecrow to rid the ship of the bird. Nevel was terrified for her; it was a long way up. She was most likely chosen because she was the smallest and Nevel knew she was agile, but he also knew after trying to scale the rock with her in the outback that climbing wasn't her strength. Nevel pushed and pulled at the sheets as David pushed the tiller, all the while watching Quinn wavering a hundred feet above and praying she would not fall.

The winds were picking up and the swells were growing. Quinn teetered at the top of the mast, shooing away the bird that kept attempting to land on it.

"Must be 15, maybe 20 knots now," David called looking up at the wind vane, "See 'em white caps off yonder?"

Nevel didn't know how to respond. He looked to the frothing sea and then back up at Quinn.

"Eh, won't be long 'till that bird gives up and yer brother can come down safe and sound." David could obviously read the fear in Nevel's eyes.

Then David pointed at the sky. The clouds were high and wispy. "That there's a mackerel sky. Change in weather soon."

"Yesterday's sky showed cat's paws and mare's tails," another sailor said. "Storm's a 'comin."

Nevel looked at Quinn and was relieved to see she had been given the signal to come back down. The bird was gone. Nevel could breathe.

Nevel could overhear the captain talking to the first mate from the deck above. "This constant north-westerly wind has kept us on track, but the wind's starting to shift southeasterly. We're going to be pushed back unless we head further out and get in a better position for this next shift in wind." The first mate nodded in agreement and then signaled for the skipper to give orders to the hands on deck.

Nevel kept an eye on Branson as he worked on the lines across the deck. It couldn't be the same Branson from the tunnel. He couldn't have been the Banded Brother who tried to attack Quinn. They were on the same watch, but hadn't interacted much. Nevel made eye contact with him several times by accident and each time his stomach twisted. Easily he could have been just another burly sailor, but the more Nevel watched him, the more Nevel felt he was being watched.

That night Quinn and Nevel were on the late watch and with the wind whipping and seas boiling, they found themselves together bailing water.

"How ya doin', sailor?" Quinn asked playfully between waves.

"I'm ok, but how are you? You ok?" Nevel was looking her over for signs of injury, but she was stronger than he gave her credit for.

"I was scared up on that mast, I won't lie," Quinn whispered, "but the view was unbelievable!"

"I thought I'd crawl out of my skin watching you climb up there," Nevel whispered back.

"It was actually the best part of my day." Quinn never ceased to surprise Nevel and he grinned at her gusto. "Can you believe this? In a day or two we will be on an island!" Quinn sounded excited.

Suddenly, Nevel lost his footing and began to slip.

"Nevel!" Quinn shouted as she scrambled to grab his ankle, causing them both to fall and slide across the wet deck uncontrollably. The ship was keeling and Nevel felt like he was on a seesaw. Abruptly, a hand grabbed him by his arm and he was lifted back up to his feet. It was David. He had grabbed Quinn with his other hand and hoisted her up so that they were both on two feet again.

"Thanks," Nevel said. Quinn just nodded. The less she spoke the better.

"Get yer sea legs ready, it's gonna be a long night," David said.

David was right. All night they fought swells that lifted and tossed the boat. The smell of rain preceded a down-pouring that was accompanied by sharp strikes of lightning and deafening thunder. Nevel stuck close to Quinn through the storm, never taking his eyes off of her as they bailed and bailed and bailed. Curtains of rain fell as they slipped and slid across an ever-moving deck. It seemed the storm would never end, but eventually the pouring rain slowed to a sprinkle and with a gust of wind, the storm blew away.

The end of the storm marked a welcome change in shifts. Nevel and Quinn's port shift went down below to dry off and eat before sleeping again. The cook had hot soup and they each went to get a bowl to bring back and drink on their bunks. Sailors were taking off wet clothes, wringing them out, and hanging them on their cots to dry. Nevel did the same with his shirt, but Quinn remained soggy—acting as if hunger trumped her desire to be dry. Chatter began as the soup brought the sailors back to life.

"I been in storms a lot tougher 'en that," David laughed as he boasted over his bowl of soup, throwing a challenge out to the crowd.

"Bloody hell, I sailed right straight through a typhoon," the sailor Nevel now knew as Shafer boasted and the banter was off and running.

Nevel sat silently with Quinn on her top bunk. Both were still soggy from the storm.

"You two related or something?" Nevel was surprised to hear Branson ask from his cot over the banter of the others.

"Yeah, we're brothers," Nevel answered, taking some more soup and hoping that would be the end of it.

"Your brother's awfully quiet," Branson probed, looking at Quinn with narrowed eyes.

"Yeah, well, he's young and we got a lot behind us," Nevel answered again.

"What the hell you doin' on a ship? Don't yer parents put ya in school or send you in the Banded Brothers?" Shafer chimed in.

"Our parents are dead. We had to find a way to feed ourselves. Heard a ship was the life, feed ya and take care of ya and you get to see the world." Nevel swallowed hard. His stomach twisted. The boat rocked.

"This ain't no babysittin' service. With all them men tryin' out for crew, how the bloody hell did you two get picked?" Now Shafer wasn't letting up.

"He speaks Filipino!" Quinn broke in in her deepest voice. Nevel wished she hadn't.

"Smart fella," Branson said and he looked at Nevel like he knew more than he should.

12

Land Ho

Nevel woke in a sweat. The heat below deck was brutal without any fresh air tunneling through. That wasn't the only reason for his sweat, though.

Nevel dreamed Branson had taken his pack. When he woke to find it still in his clutches, he was so relieved that he lay still for a few moments breathing deeply. Nevel stood in the dark and wrapped his hands around the top bunk post before pulling his weight up with his biceps to check on Quinn. She was asleep above him on her bunk. He wished he could crawl up there with her and wrap his arms around her as they had slept in the city on the fifteenth floor. Obviously, he couldn't. He returned to his bed and tried to close his eyes and sleep. He tossed and turned.

Thoughts of the Register, his brush with death at the gallows, his parents and dog, the conversation he overheard in the depository rushed through his mind and made his pulse dance uncontrollably. So much had happened and this was perhaps only the beginning of his journey. He wondered if he was strong enough to face what lay ahead for him. He worried about bringing Quinn onto a dangerous journey. He tried to calm his mind by reading inside his mind, but the words were blurry as his mind raced. Everyone around him was sleeping. He could hear the crew on deck above singing a sea chantey as the vessel glided over calm seas. He told himself over and over again, *Everything is going to be OK* and *One day at a time.* Finally his restlessness gave way to sleep.

"All hands on deck!" He heard the call and all of the sleeping sailors began to scramble to their feet. Nevel looked at Quinn. She was rubbing her tired eyes in confusion. Dawn's light was just barely breaking and creeping in through the cracks from the planks above.

"Land Ho!" he heard someone call and Nevel met Quinn's eyes with a look of wonder. They raced to the ladder and fell in line with the other sailors to head towards the top deck. At the top of the ladder, every man fell into position, but all eyes were on the view that consumed the horizon. Land lay in the distance in the form of a mountainous, beautiful green mass.

Nevel was so distracted by the sight of a new land and the thought of adventure that he didn't hear Branson's first attempt to get his attention.

"Kid, I said I know who you are." Branson

nudged him in the ribs as the line moved to hoist the sail.

Nevel's knees grew weak. He tried to gain composure. Nevel pulled at lines and nodded back at Branson.

"Yeah, so?" Nevel said, trying desperately to appear aloof.

"Your dad sent me," Branson said looking up at the whipping sail and then back over his shoulder at Nevel who continued his job pulling the lines behind him. "Said you might have a delivery for me to bring back to him?"

"Don't know what that'd be," Nevel lied. His palms dampened. His heart pounded. His gut twisted.

"You sure about that, Nevel?" Suddenly, Nevel didn't like the sound of his own name. They had agreed to use real names as they were far enough away from Morgan Creek and figured that they would never run into anyone who could connect them to their past, but now Nevel regretted the decision as his name sounded so filthy coming out of the sneering man's lips. Maybe Branson knew who he was. Nevel's mind spun. Had his father really sent Branson, not yet knowing that Branson was a threat to the UBM? Or was Branson lying about being sent by his father? Had he followed Nevel here? Nevel had tried to warn his father about Branson, but he had run out of time. Did Branson know Nevel had the Register? The only thing Nevel did know was that he had to test Branson and, if he passed, he'd have to play along.

"What's my father's name?"

"Henry Walker." Branson was on point. There

was no way for him to know this unless he was indeed *the* Branson from the depository.

"I–I'm still new to this. He didn't give me anything, just instructions to pick up something on my trip," Nevel said, keeping as calm as possible.

"Well my orders are to take whatever it is you pick up back to your dad. You see that that happens, ya hear?" was Branson's reply.

Nevel swallowed a lump in his throat and wished he hadn't left his pack unsecured on his bunk below deck.

13

Crew

The sailors were all at the lines, unlashing topsail yards and bringing the mainsail yard back into position while shackling lower topsail sheets to prepare for their trip to land. The ship keeled smoothly and slid across the surface of the ocean like a graceful swan. The captain appeared from the top deck, watching the work of the crew and nodding in agreement before turning to speak with the salt and pepper mustached officer.

Quinn was on deck duty again, which Nevel was glad of as it took little strength and allowed her to work alone without the harassment of the others. She pushed water off the deck's surface and over the edge with what looked like a long, wide mop. She had become quite agile on the boat, skipping over coils of rope and bending her knees to keep her stance at the ship's keeling. She had a dance-like manner with which she moved across the deck. Nevel had mentioned to her once or twice that she needed to be careful not to appear too flamboyant in her movements and draw attention to herself.

Nevel was in a long line of men pulling at the sheets to adjust the sails. His arms were thinner than those of the other sailors, but they were still muscular. He enjoyed the work, as he was able to feel what it was to ride the ocean and to feel the salt spray against his face. Nevel appreciated the sea chanteys the men would sing. He felt a part of something, a team of sorts. He had never been a piece of a bigger moving machine and it felt good to be included and integral in its success.

"You two, fetch the trade crates," the first mate yelled at Nevel and David who was next to him in their line. They obliged and released their ropes and went towards the center of the deck to drop below. Down below the deck, it was hot and sticky.

"The crates are over yonder," David told Nevel as they walked toward the back of the cabin where the air was even hotter and thicker. Nevel bent down to pick up a crate and thought his arms would come off before he was able to lift it off the ground. David laughed and switched places with him. The crate David switched with him was definitely more manageable and Nevel lifted it onto his right shoulder and followed David back to the center of the boat where they hoisted them up and passed them to sailors waiting above.

David easily lifted another one and passed it to Nevel who clearly struggled with its weight.

"What's in these?" Nevel asked as he managed to pass it to Shafer who waited at the top of the ladder.

"Blimey, a bunch of crap," David answered as they continued to lift and pass crates.

"Well, how do they get all the goods if they just trade a bunch of crap?" Nevel was curious.

"Damn Neanderthals don't know it's crap," David answered.

It felt good to release the crates and be relieved of their weight while catching the salt-air breeze the opening provided. Nevel was sore and hot as he passed the crates.

As they handed the last of the crates up, Nevel glanced to ensure that his pack was still in fact on his bunk. He also knew that Branson was still on deck.

"David, you mind covering for me for two minutes while I use a pot?" Nevel lied about having to use the bathroom.

"No problem, mate," David responded and was gone.

Nevel hurried to his pack. He had to hide the Register. He pulled a length of twine from under a bunk and tied the Register to his back, knowing that the two passes of the crow were tucked inside. It would only have to hold long enough to make it ashore so he could hide it. He took a knife and tucked it in his shoe. The rest of the pack he tossed on his bunk where it had been.

14

Papua New Guinea

The Lilian Ruth slowly reached her limit as she approached the shallower water leading up to the island and the anchor was dropped. The small long boats that held thirty men were loaded with the cargo to trade before being deployed. The starboard watch was to row the starboard small boat and the port watch was to row the port small boat, each carrying officers and crates of "crap," as David noted.

The boat-ride up to the island of Papua New Guinea took Nevel's breath away. Never in his life had he witnessed such raw, lush beauty. He had always seen the beauty in his home in Australia, but this was different, like nothing he had ever seen—even in the pictures in his mind. The waters in the shallows were crystal clear, so clear he could see Parrott fish nibbling on coral and flounder stirring up sand over their flat bodies on the sea floor. As the waves rippled calmly and the paddles splashed, patterns of sunlight reflected and danced on the water.

On land in the distance that was growing ever closer, tropical trees hung with coconuts. Mountains painted the backdrop; some were volcanoes with red lava tops emitting steam into the blue sky. Along the shorelines, thatched huts matched those of the books in his mind that showed scattered island villages. Possibly the most beautiful view came from the island people themselves who came out of their huts in tribal garb, displaying welcome dances at the ship's approach. The people had rich dark skin painted with white lines and circles and they were barefoot as they lifted their knees high and bent at the waist in story-telling dance.

Nevel had read about Papua New Guinea in his travel books. He knew Guinea was one of those places that was still living without technology at the time of the MegaCrash. Living in tribes and villages, the indigenous people were literally unaffected by the MegaCrash. Nevel could tell from his books that the island had previously been ignored, dismissed as behind the times before the MegaCrash. Nevel wondered if they would be treated differently now; tribal people were expert survivalists from whom the post-technological generations could learn a lot. Or would his fellow crewmembers remain pompous in their more civilized lifestyles and miss completely the wealth of lessons they could take from a people successful at living off the land? Nevel felt reverent as he looked to the islands he knew from books still had many untouched areas, new discoveries to be made, new resources to be harvested. Sure, he knew it also had an air of danger—he had read about witchcraft, black magic, and sorcery in Papua New Guinea—but he also knew that these were perhaps just the authors' interpretation of traditional indigenous practices in their rituals for health, fertility, death, and gender initiation. Nevel wondered how his ship of conquistadors would treat this gem of an island.

In the small boat, Nevel rowed behind Quinn, pulling on his oars as hard as he could to make up for her lack of upper body strength. From these boats, it was impossible to keep his eyes off the crystal clear water revealing an entire world beneath them. Coral twisted in elaborate patterns and housed brightly colored tropical fish that flitted all about. The sand bottom was easy to spot where crustaceans crawled about as if they were on land. Sea stars, anemones, and seaweed dug in the sand bottom as the boats floated over, unaware of the world above them. As the boats grew closer, Nevel could hear the tribal drums playing and could better see these people who danced to greet them.

Nevel was shocked at what he saw. These people had bones ornamentally woven through their noses. They wore grass skirts and leaves over their bodies. They wore shelled necklaces and leg-ties. They looked just like the people he had read about in history books. His mouth gaped as he looked at what appeared to be a page from a history book come to life.

He couldn't take his eyes off of them. It was as if time didn't pass here.

The paddles began brushing the sand below the water and finally the boat was stopped by the ground beneath it. The crew stepped out into shallow water and pulled the boats the rest of the way to dry sand where officers disembarked into the strange, new world. The language was like nothing Nevel had ever heard. He could not translate it with any book in his head. The officers had clearly traded here before as they used gestures to communicate. A crate was opened and the tribal peoples gawked. Nevel was embarrassed as he beheld the contents of the crate he had helped load and bring ashore.

It was full of old cell phones and keyboards and digital tablets that were useless in this post-technological era. The tribal peoples clearly did not know this and began offering coconuts, bananas, and woven baskets to trade. Nevel stood and watched, embarrassed at the act of fraud.

Still, Nevel was in awe of the scene. The strangest part wasn't their tribal, prehistoric appearance or their ancient undocumented languages. The strangest part was how the MegaCrash hadn't changed their lives at all. Their today was a yesterday so far back that Nevel only knew of it from books in his mind. Nevel had read of the variety of natives that had been historically documented within the impenetrable rainforests and ragged mountain mazes of New Guinea. There were rumors of thousands of languages, pygmies and giants, hidden valleys, and even sacrifices. Nevel wondered if these accounts from long ago in the books in his mind were still accurate about the tribes of today. He certainly couldn't see why they wouldn't be; he was living a page in a history book right now as he stood on the sand in a tribal village and watched a people who were unchanged by the MegaCrash.

Three tribal men broke into a loud, calling song that reverberated through the swaying palms. Moments later, boys appeared from the edge of the jungle with handfuls of fruits and greens. They didn't need cell phones, Nevel thought, they called each other with songs. Nevel watched as the tribal peoples worked to produce more and more offerings for trade before his very eyes. They didn't need the modern items that so many Australians had missed since the MegaCrash to survive. They cut and cooked and wove before his very eyes with only rudimentary objects found on their island. Nevel couldn't imagine why they would trade for the junk presented to them, but he knew shiny foreign objects like nothing ever created in nature would be revered just by their pure oddity.

Nevel walked to where Quinn was accepting a coconut from a tribal child. He whispered in her ear. "There is a crew member who is onto us."

"What? Who?" Quinn was confused.

"Branson." As Nevel said his name, he and Quinn both looked up and were caught by Branson's returned glance.

Trickles of nervous sweat beaded on Nevel's forehead and dripped down Nevel's back where the Register was hidden beneath his shirt.

15

Alone

The captain told the crew that the trades would keep the ship and her crew on land overnight. Nevel learned from the chatter on board that many of the sailors would find love overnight while others would drink themselves into oblivion. There were no rules for the ship's crew for the night. The only orders given were to be prepared to return to the ship just after sunrise or risk being stuck on the island forever. The Lilian Ruth would wait for no man.

This would be Nevel and Quinn's first chance to be alone since living in the city.

"Let's go," Quinn whispered as she cocked her head and pointed up the beach. Nevel checked to be sure no one was watching them. There was so much commotion with the trades and the dancing and the bonfires and singing that they easily slipped away unnoticed.

They ran down the beach at least a mile until it turned a hard right and surprised them completely. A coral reef that was visible from land stretched out right across the water as far as they could see from the straight stretch of beach, forming an aqua-colored lagoon tucked in the bend and lined by white sand and waving palms. It was beautiful. Nevel looked at Quinn and she let out a squeal of delight as they ran all the way to the bend to take in their paradise found. As soon as he was convinced they were out of sight, Nevel wrapped his arms around Quinn's waist and pulled her in close to him. He kissed her with a passion that had been building for days. His lips on hers made him feel electrified and the thrill of their adventure in this tropical paradise rushed through his body. He lifted her up, still kissing her. She ran her hands through his hair knotted from the sea winds and kissed him with equal passion. Then the kiss was interrupted as Quinn's hands reached around Nevel's back and felt the book.

"What's that?" she asked, confused as she pulled away.

"Yeah, there's something I need to tell you," Nevel filled her in about the voices he had heard in their depository in the outback. He also told her about the fact that one voice he had heard in the caves connecting to the depository had somehow resurfaced here. He asked her if she noticed that her attacker from the city had the same tattoo. Nevel also told her about the conversation he had shared with Branson on the boat that morning.

"Wow," Quinn said as she stared out at the sea, "I had no idea."

"It's something we will have to deal with, but for now it can wait."

Nevel pulled the register from his back and looked around for a place to stash it. He quickly made his way to a palm tree and climbed to a vee in its trunk then lifted the book high to lay it on a wide, flat palm leaf above. He jogged back to where Quinn was on the beach.

"There, now we can forget about it for a little bit and enjoy ourselves!" With these words, Nevel could almost see a light ignite in Quinn's eyes.

"Look at us, on an island! I never dreamed I would be in a place like this." Quinn smiled and took Nevel's hand.

"Unbelievable! It's better than any picture I've seen in any book," Nevel replied looking out across the blue lagoon in this tropical paradise.

"And I'm glad to see you're still attracted to me with my short hair and boy disguise," Quinn said, checking Nevel's eyes for a sincere response.

Nevel laughed, brushing her hair out of her face with a smile, but then said frankly, "You are more beautiful than anything I have ever seen."

Quinn seemed embarrassed at his compliment and turned to the water. "Nothing could be more beautiful than this," she said as they both looked out into a lagoon where sea life blossomed in vibrant colors. Pinks, oranges, and browns of coral trellised a border that made the lagoon the private, calm pool that it was. Greens of seaweed swayed in the underwater ebbs and flows. Stripes and spots and leopard patterns in rich yellows and blacks and purples adorned fish of all shapes and sizes that darted safely about, without any fear of their larger predators that lurked in deeper waters. The cool pure water was inviting. Nevel was hot and had been so confined in the city and then below deck of the ship that he took in one long deep breath and felt his lungs would explode with the fresh freedom he finally was given. It was hard to take his eyes off of the glass menagerie of the sea, but he finally turned to look at Quinn to see her reaction to this magical place.

She just stared at the water, like she was looking into a crystal ball or something, like it was showing her what was to come. Nevel wondered what she was thinking. While he was identifying species of fish as he looked at the sea, she was probably remembering summers with her family before the world changed. She had been in water before. Had it been this beautiful? Had she seen fish like these?

They were still in their sailor uniforms: white pants and white shirts with navy stitching, and rubber soled shoes, which were now heavy with sand. Quinn kicked her shoes off and walked toward the water. Nevel did the same.

The soft sand under foot was interrupted by something sharp piercing his arch. He lifted his foot to reveal a large conch shell.

"Look at this!" Nevel shouted in excitement. Without even waiting for Quinn's response, Nevel dropped to his knees in the sand and started picking up shell after shell after shell.

"Conchs! Scotch bonnets! Sea glass!" Nevel was astonished at the sheer number of shells all around him—for the taking! Every beach he had seen so far had been stripped of its treasures. Finally, Nevel found out what it was to be a shell collector. He held out his shirt like a bowl and began filling it with shells.

"What are you going to do with all those shells, Bookkeeper?" Quinn teased and Nevel laughed and rolled his eyes before going back to his treasure hunt.

"Look at how blue that water is," she said, awestruck as she folded herself at the waist to bend and dip her finger in it, almost as if she were checking to see if it were real. The water that was beginning to lap at their ankles was making their pants translucent as the fabric stuck to their legs like a second, new skin.

"Water is funny that way," Nevel joked as he poured his shell collection from his shirt into a pile on the dry sand, "always blue and never red or black or..."

"Really, Nevel?" Quinn seemed offended as she stood to face him. "What color is water at night? Black like the sky!" She tossed her hands as she spoke adamantly about her subject. "What color is water under a rain cloud? Sometimes grey! And how about water that picks up the green hues of the algae?"

"Whoa." Nevel backed up with his palms up in surrender and smirked. "I didn't mean to make you mad!"

Quinn spun around on the sand to face the sea and

crossed her arms on her chest. "Sometimes, Nevel, life isn't just made of facts. You act like you know everything because of those books in your brain, but you don't know everything." She turned back around to look at Nevel who was now furrowing his eyebrows as he ran his hands through his wavy locks. "Sometimes you have to live things, experience them for yourself to see something more. You don't know everything."

Porpoises broke the surface of the water a few yards outside the lagoon in the low rolling waves of the deeper water and a wide grin painted itself across Quinn's face. Nevel looked at her, still a bit confused. She was right, he thought, he didn't know everything.

After a few moments, Quinn took a deep breath and shook off whatever was on her mind. She turned to him. "Wanna try your water wings?" Quinn challenged waving her arms like a bird and walking backwards into the shallow lagoon.

"What if I sink?" Nevel laughed nervously as he followed her to the water. She continued stepping backwards, eyes locked on Nevel, as he proceeded forward. They were ankle deep, then knee deep, and suddenly waist deep when Quinn turned and dove under. Her sailor suit stuck and flopped and showed the bandage still wrapped around Quinn's chest. Nevel waded a bit further. The water was cool and refreshing as it now hit his chest. He felt the slime and scum of the voyage slipping off of every inch of him that became covered by water. Quinn surfaced a few feet ahead. Her red hair slicked back gave emphasis to her beautifully sculpted face. Her green eyes sparkled and her wide smile made his heart skip a beat.

"Come on," she called, treading water, "give it a try. I'll save you if you start to drown."

She laughed and Nevel smirked at her making light of his possible impending doom. He wanted to try it. He had always wanted to try it.

Nevel knew it was shallow enough that he could stand again if he wasn't able to keep himself afloat. He took a long breath and lifted his feet from the bottom for a moment before instinctively putting them right back on the sandy ground again to support his weight. He tried again, lifting his knees up to his chest, trying to push the water down with his hands to keep himself up. At first he did not succeed and he had to once again land on his feet.

"Make big circles with your arms," Quinn called as she treaded water and watched with a wide grin before swimming back towards him. He tried again and finally found himself supporting his weight with his arms making figure eights. He continued to lean on the crutch of the sandy bottom beneath him when his head got close to dipping under, but soon realized he was in fact able to keep himself afloat.

"Now try lying on your stomach with your feet behind you. Kick your feet and move your arms in circles stretched out in front of you." Quinn was showing him and made it look easy. Nevel mimicked her actions and swallowed saltwater. "Ok, try again. This time start at your chest and push two circles out and back to start." She showed him and he tried, but still coughed water.

"Hold your breath, crazy!" Quinn laughed and

Nevel was embarrassed. He tried again. Before he knew it, he was moving through the water, awkwardly, but afloat.

"You're doing it!" Quinn called as she swam to him.

"I look pretty tough," Nevel laughed and Quinn burst into hysterical laughter.

"Try spreading your arms and make wider circles and keep your fingers together so your hands push the water like cups." She swam graceful circles around him. Nevel imitated her moves, although not nearly as gracefully. She swam and he followed. His mind temporarily forgot about swimming as he just wanted to get to her. Suddenly he was swimming. It reminded him of learning to ride a bike. He remembered his dad holding onto the back as he had wobbled up and down the dirt road in front of his house. He fell to the left or right every time his dad let go, but when his dad started asking him questions and distracting him, he was suddenly riding the bike without even realizing his dad had let go.

It felt amazing to be free of his body's weight in the water. The tightness of his muscles loosened and he let his arms and legs be moved by the water. Quinn let him catch up to her in a place where they could stand chest-deep and wrapped her arms around him. They kissed in the lagoon in their own private paradise.

Nevel was disappointed when Quinn quickly pulled away. He didn't want the moment to end.

"I don't think we're alone," Quinn whispered.

16
Cover

Branson stood on the shore watching Nevel and Quinn. Quickly, the two broke apart from one another.

"Oh no," Quinn gasped, "Do you think he saw us kiss...our cover is blown!"

"Stay here, in the water," Nevel said coolly as he started for the beach.

Nevel's heart pounded harder the closer he grew to the beach. Branson stood waiting, arms crossed atop his chest and a smirk on his face. Nevel walked from the waves, his uniform thin and wet and pressed on his skin. Drops of saltwater were raining down his body.

"What do you want?" Nevel asked without a smile.

"You have something I am supposed to take off your hands," Branson replied.

"I told you, I don't." Nevel shook his wet hair in an attempt to dry off.

"I'm not buying it," Branson said, and then his eyes scanned to Quinn in the water. "She's not who you think she is, you know."

"What are you talking about? I don't know what you think you saw, but..." Nevel tried desperately to make sense of it all, for Quinn's sake.

"Don't," Branson interjected. He was standing firm on the sand and his scruffy face was inches from Nevel's. His breath smelled of rotting teeth. His finger was pointing and pressing in Nevel's chest at every point he emphasized. "I'm just telling you *I* know a lot more than you think. *I* know she ain't a he and *I* know that ain't her only secret and *I* know you got something I'm supposed to be takin' back to your dad."

"And why wouldn't I just take it back to him?"

"'Cause you ain't goin' back!"

Nevel didn't know if Branson's exclamation was a threat or a fact. Did Branson know what the UBM had planned for Nevel? He kicked at the sand and struggled to find words, "And If I don't have what you're looking for? What are you gonna do about it?"

Now Branson looked him square in the eyes, teeth clenched. "I'm gonna give you till mornin' to figure out what you're gonna do about it." And he turned and walked away, back toward the camp the sailors had set up upon landing earlier.

A wet Quinn joined a stunned Nevel on shore. She

was shaking the water off of her arms and hair as she approached.

"He knows," Nevel offered and sat on the dry sand with his elbows around his bent knees, looking defeated.

"What does he know?" Quinn sat next to him on the warm sand.

"Everything—that you're a girl, who I am—he says my dad sent him. He knows I've got the Register." Nevel looked out at the sea as he talked. He was lost.

"Bloody hell." Quinn put a hand on Nevel's knee.

"Yeah, he was in Morgan Creek. He pretends to be UBM, but I know he is connected to the government somehow." Nevel was deep in thought.

"Then he knows about our trial, our escape..." Quinn traced circles in the sand with her index finger.

"Yep." Nevel stretched his feet out and threw a shell into the water. The shell skipped twice on the water's surface before sinking into it.

"But he doesn't know you're a bookkeeper..." Quinn looked at Nevel who was picking up another shell and sending it skipping.

"Who knows?" He stopped to look at her. "He said something about you not being who I think you are."

Quinn shifted in the sand and rolled her eyes, "I guess he knows I'm Driscoll's daughter too then."

"It doesn't make sense. How would he know that? I mean, you didn't even know that until you chased me into the bloody outback and held a knife to my throat." Nevel tried to meet her eyes, but she stood up and started shaking the sand from her wet pants.

"He's full of it," she said and started walking back to the water. Nevel wondered what it could mean. He wondered what he would do. How would they re-board the ship with a man who knew all of their secrets? Would he have to give him the Register to keep him quiet?

Quinn dove back into the blue water, washing the sand clear off her white suit. She looked like one of the porpoises as she dipped up and down across the water's surface with grace. Nevel stood and walked to the water's edge. He would have to protect the Register, the UBM, his Quinn. Nevel didn't know where their journey would take them from here. He was waiting to find out where the UBM would send him. The ship would island hop for a while for trade, but eventually it would return to Australia. Nevel didn't know whether he would be returning to Australia with it. He knew he could never return to Morgan Creek and he could never live in Brisbane, but Australia was a big place. No matter what, Nevel knew that Branson couldn't return to Australia knowing so much and threatening the UBM and his father. He would have to get rid of Branson before the morning.

17
Plan

On the beach, Nevel summoned Quinn to shore with a waving hand. She walked to him, shaking her wet ragged hair with her hands to dry it. Nevel had his hands on his hips and a plan in his mind.

"I'm going to meet Branson," Nevel announced. Quinn didn't look surprised.

"And? What do you plan to do when you meet him?" Quinn wrung the water out of her shirt by twisting it up on the sides, exposing her slender waist.

"I'm going to tell him I have a package for him, lead him into the jungle, and tie him to a tree. He'll be left behind when we set sail in the morning." Nevel's words were not coated in confidence. He sounded nervous, like he was just sharing this plan with himself as the words fell from his lips.

"Simple enough," Quinn winked and looked down the beach where the Lilian Ruth waited at sea. "So we go now?"

"*I* go," Nevel said. "You stay here. I will come back for you tonight. Just lay low."

"Don't you think you could use some help?" Quinn said and he knew she was right, but he didn't want to risk her getting hurt. He could handle this on his own.

"You stay here and guard the Register. I'll be back in a few hours."

Nevel went to the tree to check that the Register was still there. It was. A fork in the branches held it tight. He picked up his shoes and pulled the knife out of the left shoe and gripped it in his right hand. Quinn watched him put the shoes on and she looked worried.

"You sure about this, bookkeeper?" She had her head tilted to catch his eyes, which were looking down at his shoes.

"Yep," Nevel lied. "Stay here and I'll be back before dark."

With that, Nevel took off in a slow jog up the beach toward the crew of the Lilian Ruth. He slowed to a walk as he reached the thatched huts, which were surrounded by tribal people and sailors in mobs looking at various objects, singing, laughing, and drinking from coconuts. Nevel scanned the crowd for Branson. He saw David chewing on a stick of sugarcane. He saw Shafer shoving bananas into his mouth. He saw the captain talking to the tribal chief through hand gestures. Finally, Nevel's eyes fell on Branson who was standing by a native woman and stroking her cheek creepily with the back of his rough hand.

Nevel walked to him. "I got that package."

Branson looked irritated to be interrupted during his flirting, but turned to Nevel anyway. "Yeah? Where is it?"

"I'll take you to it." Nevel motioned toward the jungle with his head.

Branson looked at him with narrowed eyes, possibly doubting him for the moment, but then seemed to remember his goal and left the woman's side to follow Nevel into the jungle.

"This better be quick," he grumbled as they began their trek through thick vines and over soggy, lush green groundcover.

"It's just a little ways in," Nevel lied as he led his victim to the unknown.

Nevel wished he still had his pack that lay waiting for him on his bunk on the ship. Inside the pack, he had rope. Here, he did not. As he pushed back more vines to further penetrate the wilderness, Nevel realized the vines would be his rope in this jungle.

"Glad you came around, mate." Branson spat on the jungle floor and trampled over a beautiful tropical flower. "What kind of package we talkin' about?" he asked gruffly as he trudged on, swatting at mosquitoes and vines.

"All I know is it's UBM. I stuck it in a tree just a ways further."

"It have a big R on the front?" Branson asked and Nevel knew now it was the Register he was after. Branson was underestimating Nevel. He must have thought Nevel believed his father really sent him. He must have thought they were on the same side. Nevel wanted to laugh at the fact that Branson was clueless to what was really going on.

"Yep," Nevel said, still moving deeper and deeper into the jungle. He turned to look at Branson over his shoulder. Branson was sweating like a pig, but had a grin on his face at the thought of growing nearer to the Register.

Now was the time for Nevel to set the trap. He stopped at a large merbau tree and looked up.

"Why did you stick it in a tree?" a breathless Branson huffed. "Well go the bloody hell up and get it."

Nevel looked up at the tree and back at Branson. He then started scratching at his ankle as if he was fighting off ants. "Bloody ants. It's just in the crook of that branch." Nevel pointed at a branch and pulled at a vine that hung nearby. As Branson walked to the branch, Nevel began pulling at more vines. Branson's eyes were in search of the prize and he didn't notice Nevel walking a circle around the tree, wrapping the vines. Branson reached. Nevel pulled. The vines tightened and in a second bound a startled Branson to the tree.

"What the..." Branson struggled as Nevel pulled and wrapped faster and faster, tying Branson so that he was hugging the tree.

"I'm gonna kill you, boy," Branson warned as he attempted to pull away from the tree to no avail. Nevel wrapped again and again with the thick vines, twisting them and braiding them before finally tying them in a knot through a loop in a massive tree branch until he was convinced Branson could not break free. Nevel started to walk away, checking over his shoulder nervously. He was covered in sweat and his hands were shaking.

"You think you're smart," Branson called after him. "You don't even know who that girl really is!"

Nevel stopped in his tracks. Yes he did, he knew Quinn better than anyone. Why did Branson keep saying that? He ignored it and walked on. Branson continued screaming, but Nevel knew they were too far from the beach now for anyone to hear him. The further he walked, the quieter the screams hung in the distance. The vines would hold him until tomorrow and the Lilian Ruth would wait for no man.

Nevel walked back toward the beach, retracing the path they had tromped on their way in. Nevel pulled at vines several times to cover his tracks just in case. Suddenly he began to feel an insatiable itch on his left calf. He stopped to scratch his leg. He reached down and pulled up his white pant leg to find what appeared to be dozens of red bumps—ant bites, he figured. They itched and burned, but as his finger nails dug into his skin, he heard a sound other than the distant screams of Branson. There was movement, rustling not far from him. He quietly moved behind a tree, holding his breath. He peered out from behind the tree, careful not to make a sound. In the distance, near where Branson was tied to a tree, a white flash went by. It was another sailor. Had they been followed? Was someone already setting Branson free? The white flashed by again and was interrupted only by the

110

greens of the jungle and one other color. One color
atop the person's head was unmistakable; it was red.

18

Screams

The sound of a man's blood curdling screams echoed through the jungle. "Monkeys, just monkeys," Nevel told himself, but his stomach twisted. He knew he had seen Quinn. He would go back to their lagoon and confront her there, not here where he was too near Branson.

Nevel returned to the lagoon and wasn't surprised that he did not find Quinn there. He began to pull at large palms to make a bed for the night at the edge of the beach so they would have a place to sleep when she returned. The sun was beginning to go down and he was irritated that she had not yet returned. He knew she would be here any minute and so he waited, continuing to place palms and even grabbing a few coconuts to eat when she came back. But where was she? He was ready to berate her for following him into the jungle. Didn't she trust that he could do a thing so simple as to tie a man to a tree? Now she had put herself in a dangerous situation for no reason. The task was done. Where was she?

The darkness of night reached over the island and seemed to swallow it whole. Nevel sat in blackness and began to feel less angry at Quinn and more concerned for her well-being. Barking sounds, chirps, and hisses filled his ears. The jungle was a different beast at night; it came alive with glowing eyes and eerie sounds. He regretted not confronting Quinn in the jungle earlier. He paced back and forth on the beach, constantly looking over his shoulder into the jungle behind him then back down the stretch of beach to where the Lilian Ruth waited, terrified at every second that she wasn't there. He tried to stop his mind from flashing across the pages in the travel books he had read about this island, about jaguars that stalked at night, poisonous snakes, and spiders that could kill with one bite.

It was really dark. Nevel sat on the bed of palms and stared out at the water. She was right. The water wasn't blue anymore, it was as black as the night and it looked like a moving black asphalt highway coming for him again and again. Nevel no longer had his flint and steel. He couldn't make fire. He could see bonfires and torches along the beach in the distance where the crew from the Lilian Ruth enjoyed their island night. Every now and then, the wind blew in his direction and carried the bantering and tribal drumbeats to his ears.

Hours passed and still no Quinn. Nevel stood up and walked to the jungle's edge. It was dark and full of noises that were different from those of the beach. It was the same jungle, but he would never find his way from here to there through its thick and twisted mazes. He would have to go in after her, but from the entrance near the Lilian Ruth.

He put on his shoes and went to the tree where he had left the Register with the Passes of the Crow still tucked safely inside. He had to bring it with him; he couldn't leave something so valuable unguarded. He tucked it in his pants and took off towards the bonfires. Nevel jogged along the beach towards the bonfires and huts where the crew was singing raucously and no doubt drinking island-made rum. The more he ran, the more the Register slipped and the more frequently he had to stop to adjust it. He didn't want it to hinder him in his search for Quinn in the jungle. He decided to tuck it back into a tree near the tribal village where he could pick it back up before they boarded the boat in the morning. As he grew closer to the thatched huts and bonfires, he slipped to the edge of the beach where it met the jungle and tucked the Register in the crook of a tree branch high above his head as he had done in their lagoon. With the Register no longer hindering his movement, he found the entrance to the jungle he had taken earlier with Branson and slipped into its darkness without ever being noticed by the boisterous crew and lively natives. As he moved through the jungle, retracing his steps from earlier, he grew nervous. He didn't want to go near

Branson—it was risky—but he had no choice.

Nevel moved along the path, brushing back vines and stamping on ferns in the dark. He was lucky the moon was bright as it helped him see his path. In the darkness of the jungle, Nevel tried to use his memory to guide him more than his eyes. His eyes made everything look too similar. After a few barking sounds and growls from the jungle's deep unknown, Nevel started jogging, tripping occasionally over vines and logs. He could feel more burning from insect bites, but he ignored them and moved on. The jungle was alive with sounds: frogs, monkeys, and the occasional growling sound which terrified Nevel but did not inhibit his movement. He had to find Quinn. Faster and faster, Nevel ran blindly through the jungle.

He knew he was coming closer to the tree where Branson was tied and so he slowed to a quiet walk. The moon peered in as the trees were larger in this portion of the jungle and more spread out. Nevel could see a bit and slowly used his mind to retrace his steps as he grew closer and closer to Branson's tree.

He was surprised he didn't hear Branson shouting or struggling about. He worried Branson may not be there anymore at all as the silence pervaded. But then the moonlight sliced through the branches, revealing the shadow of the large tree trunk with an unnatural bulge that Nevel knew must be Branson, still tied to the tree.

Nevel moved quietly toward Branson. He was still and his head was tilted to one side. Nevel figured he must be asleep so he circled around to look at Branson safely from the dark brush.

Nevel's vantage point and the moonlight allowed him to see the face that was indeed Branson's, but he was not asleep. His eyes were wide open. A shadow covered the bottom half of his face and Nevel was confused. How was he so still? Nevel watched. Branson did not blink. Nevel made a rustling sound by moving the bush a bit. Branson did not move. Nevel burst out of his hiding place but Branson remained still. Close up now, Nevel could see why.

Branson was dead.

19
Flies

His throat had been sliced wide open. Dried blood stained his white sailor suit from chest to waist and down his left leg. Flies and maggots were swarming the stale open wound. Nevel gagged and turned away, pulling his face into his elbow. He took two long breaths in his elbow and then turned his face back to look again to make sure his mind wasn't playing tricks on him. It wasn't. Nevel was staring at a dead man.

Nevel took off running into the jungle. He didn't know where he was going, just away from Branson. He didn't like the places his mind was taking him. Nevel had never seen a dead man. Quinn had been there. She must have killed him, but why? The task of preventing him from following them was done!

Nevel's cheeks felt hot. His legs were carrying him quickly through a maze of vines and palms. The eerie sounds of the jungle echoed in his ears. A thump sent him falling forward. He had tripped over a fallen tree and was face first on the soggy jungle floor. And then a sound carried across the jungle and landed right in his ear.

"CAWCAW!"

Could it be? The crow was not native to this island. Was Quinn calling for help? This had been their signal to each other—they had called each other in the outback and in Shantytown when they were captives. No, it must be his mind playing tricks on him.

"Cawcaw."

It was fainter now, but distinct—their distress call. Quinn was near.

Nevel stood and shook the dirt and leaves from himself and returned the call. "CAWCAW!" he shouted into the pitch black of night.

It was his instinctive response, forgetting about what he had seen of Branson, forgetting the suspicion that had surged within him. He followed it into the jungle to find his Quinn.

Nevel ran and repeated the call several times. Each time a faint response gave him a clue as to which direction to head until finally he came to a clearing. The moon shone on a copper-colored, muddy stream that was about eight feet across as it rushed through the jungle and twisted off into the distance. At the edge lay Quinn. Nevel rushed to her.

"Quinn, are you ok?" Quinn's body was on its

side. Her white sailor suit was stained with blood from head to toe, but the stains were wet and rinsed by the stream. Her face was pale and she appeared lifeless.

"What happened to you?" Nevel asked as he sat on the ground and pulled her body into his lap, looking her over for injuries.

Quinn's vacant eyes slowly rolled up and met Nevel's frantic look. Her lips curled into a slow grin before quickly falling limp again. Nevel found no injuries on her head or midsection or arms. Why was there so much blood? Was it Branson's? She tried to swallow and looked as if she was trying to say something.

"I got bit." Quinn pointed at her ankle. Now he saw the source of her problems. The flesh outside her right ankle was torn open and frothing.

"Oh no, what happened? What was it?" Nevel swatted the flies that surrounded her ankle to try to get a better look and accidentally brushed it with the back of his hand, making her wince in pain. Nevel knew by the books he had read that exposed wounds like this could take only a few hours to become badly infected and hers seemed to be just that.

She spoke slowly and quietly. Her breaths were labored, pants almost. Nevel was taking off his shirt and tying it as a tunicate around her wound to stop the bleeding and close it off from the flies and other dangers of the jungle. He placed the back of his hand to her forehead; she was burning up. He looked at her glazed eyes and tried to hold her attention, but her eyes rolled in and out of focus on his face.

"I was in a stream. It was so cool. The water was splashing," she panted.

Panic was growing in Nevel.

"What happened to your ankle?" Nevel demanded.

"It tickled at first," Quinn gasped. "Little fish swimming around me." Her skin was turning gray and was covered in chill bumps despite the hot fever. "I didn't know, Nevel. I didn't know little fish like that would bite." Drool spilled from the corner of her mouth.

Now Nevel knew what had happened. Quinn must have stopped at the stream to rinse Branson's blood from her hands and clothes. The blood attracted the predators that gave her this wound: Piranhas.

20

Live

There was not much night left. Nevel had to save Quinn. Again he scoured the books in his mind, disappointed to find that no natural remedy or holistic treatment would do at this stage in the infection. He couldn't help her on his own. Her wound was too badly infected. Too much time had passed; antibiotics were the only remedy at this point. Nevel guessed she had laid here now for over four hours. He knew he would have to take her to the crew of the Lilian Ruth and beg for mercy. He picked her up and began running with her in his arms back to the beach as the sun came up, as if chasing him out of the jungle.

She was heavy, but Nevel was strong. He stumbled every now and then, bumping into trees and tripping on vines in dark. He tried to keep his gait steady so as not to jostle her around any more than necessary. He also tried to talk to her to keep her awake.

"We'll be at the beach in just a bit, Quinn," Nevel said between breaths, "They'll fix you right up."

"No they won't," she laughed deliriously, but Nevel knew she was right. Why would they care to save her? Nevel knew her ankle could have easily been sewn shut if he had found her sooner, but lying on the floor of the jungle for that long bleeding had invited infection. How could he have left her in the jungle for so long? Nevel blamed himself.

"You'll be fixed up in no time. How about that moon?" Nevel tried to distract her as he ran on with her limp in his arms. He couldn't do this without her. He didn't want to do this without her. But what had she done? Was he a fool to save her? He couldn't think of that now. For now, he must think of her as his Quinn. He must save her.

"I'm not a cat, Nevel." Quinn choked a bit as she talked. "I haven't been given nine lives."

"Quit your crazy talk." Nevel ran on.

"I already beat death once," she replied through trembling lips. "I don't expect to beat it again." Her eyes rolled back in her head like she was falling asleep, but her eyelids didn't close.

Nevel was scared. He didn't want her to die. His mind raced faster than his feet through every medical book in his mind. They all told him what he was afraid to know. She needed antibiotics.

"Don't say that, Quinn. You're not going to die," Nevel tried to reassure her, but he sounded like he was reassuring himself when the words fell from his lips. Daylight was breaking and he could see a clearing ahead. They were almost to the beach.

"I'm not worried about dying, Nevel," she sputtered between breaths. "I just wasn't finished helping you learn how to live."

"We're here, Quinn, we're here." Nevel broke out of the dense jungle and onto the quiet beach where the sun was just now spreading its light.

21

Captain

Nevel knew that since the MegaCrash, only the people in the highest positions in society still held antibiotics that had been carefully saved or created painstakingly based on history's lessons. Quinn's infection was killing her. Only an antibiotic could save her. Only a captain of a ship would have antibiotics. Nevel would have to go to the captain.

The beach was quiet. Sailors lay asleep on the sand. Nevel scanned the area for the whereabouts of the captain. He saw crewmembers asleep on the sand, hands still clutching coconut husks, which he knew, had probably housed homemade rum from the night before. The several thatched huts had their doors closed. One was guarded by two sailors who were sitting on the ground asleep on either side of the door. Nevel knew this must be where the captain stayed.

Sweating and aching, Nevel dragged himself and the ever-heavier Quinn towards the hut. Unaware of his footing, Nevel stumbled over a pile of ash and branches, surely one of the bonfires from the night before. He caught himself by sacrificing his knees, protecting Quinn on the way down so she landed softly on the sand. Nevel was terrified to find that her eyes were closed now and she appeared to be asleep. He immediately checked her pulse on her neck. It was still there, but was slow and faint. Nevel cried out, "Help!" He broke the morning silence, but he didn't care. Tears began to fall from his eyes, "Help, please," he wasn't worried about the register. He wasn't worried about the UBM. He wasn't worried about giving himself away as a bookkeeper. He would do anything to save her.

Several sleepy sailors woke and got up from where they lay in the sand, walking over to him, scratching their heads and rubbing their eyes. Shafer was one.

"What the hell happened to him?" Shafer asked, insincere.

"Captain!" Nevel yelled.

David rushed over, "Hush, boy! What are you doin?" He looked at Quinn and then understood.

"My brother will die if he doesn't get help!" Nevel tried to remain in character. He would do whatever it took to get Quinn help.

"Well, shoutin' at the captain will just getcha killed," David warned and paced back and forth. The other sailors had walked away, not caring if Quinn lived or died.

"What can I do?" Nevel looked at David through teary eyes, "What else can I do? He needs antibiotics."

"Shew, you can forget it." David shook his head left to right a few times, still pacing. "You ain't gonna get it. I'm sorry, boy, but we ain't exactly antibiotic worthy if ya know what I mean. Folks like us are left to die sometimes. I'm sorry, but you're gonna lose yer brother."

Nevel was shaking now. He didn't realize the captain had heard the commotion and had come out of the hut to see what the fuss was about. Nevel looked up and saw him and pleaded his case.

"Captain, my brother! He'll die!" Nevel was desperate. He knew the risk. It could mean trouble for them both, but if he didn't try she would most certainly die.

"Why do you think our captain would care?" the first mate who stood at the captain's side dismissively spoke. He was right; Nevel had not thought this through. Why would the captain waste antibiotics on a frail crewman that was a dime a dozen?

"But I won't leave without him!" Nevel cried, tears streaming down his face. "I speak Filipino, remember? I can help with the trades."

"We've faired just fine in the past without a translator. We did it here, didn't we?" the first mate scoffed. The captain simply stood and stared; he made no move, no comment.

Nevel slowly pulled himself from his knees to

stand before the captain, holding a lifeless Quinn to his chest and sobbing out loud.

"I beg you to help him, sir. I can give you information."

What Nevel hadn't noticed was that, despite the passivity of the officers, the captain did appear empathetic as he watched Nevel's heart breaking on the sand.

"Tell me your name," the captain said to Nevel.

A world of sorrow was crushing down on Nevel. He had given up hope. He looked up and spoke between sobs, "I am Nevel Oswold Walker."

Nevel prepared for what he would have to say next, he would give anything to save Quinn. He would tell the captain that he was indeed a bookkeeper. It was the last card he held in his hand. It would mean the end for Nevel and Quinn. Nevel would become this captain's key to the world at large. Quinn would be spared, but she would not be kept on as crew for long. Her secret would be out as well. Still, it was his only chance to save her life.

Before Nevel could speak his truth, the captain gave orders. "Go and get the antibiotics," he demanded to the first mate. "Immediately."

"But, sir, we are under strict orders to use those items only to save our captain."

"DO NOT disobey my orders!" the captain screamed with a growing redness in his cheeks.

"But, Captain, we are ordered by command above your rank not to use those items on anyone but the captain." The first mate was standing his ground. Nevel was confused at the Captain's motives, but he finally had a glimpse of hope.

"This young man is my blood—the blood of your captain! Now you see? Your orders remain. Go and get the antibiotics."

The first mate stood a moment, possibly attempting to make sense of it, but then turned to quickly board a small rowboat with three crewmen to row him to the ship. "And make haste!" the captain called as the small boat took off towards the Lilian Ruth.

Nevel looked at the captain in disbelief, tears still streaming as he struggled to remain standing while holding his dying Quinn. Nevel crumbled from his standing position and landed with a thud on his rear end in the sand with Quinn still in his arms. He didn't understand. Were they related? The captain knelt by him and looked Nevel straight in the eyes.

"Sir, I apologize for not knowing. Are we kin?" Nevel asked between tears and choppy breaths. Nevel brushed away the tears with the back of his palm and sand stuck to the edges of his eyelids.

"We are brothers of sorts," the captain answered quietly. "You brought me something, didn't you?" the captain asked in a whisper.

Nevel was confused. His arms were shaking, trembling. Quinn's body was pale. He looked at her and his heart ached. He looked back to the captain, trying to stay focused. "Sir?" Nevel asked between breaths.

"The Register, son," the captain said softly.

"Of course, yes." Nevel's mind spun. The captain was UBM! Or was he? At this point, it didn't matter anymore. Nevel would have given anything to save

Quinn. "Yes, sir. I—I hid it in the tree. It's right over there." Nevel pointed to the tree on the beach that was waving its palms in the wind. "It's in the crook of the branch."

The captain walked to the tree and inspected it, not calling attention to himself. He reached up and pulled the book down, quickly tucking it under his uniformed arm. He walked back to Nevel.

"Well done. You can send word that it is safe and on it's way to its next destination." And then the captain shook Nevel's hand with the secret handshake of the UBM.

"But won't we be going with you?" Nevel was confused.

"They have other plans for you," The captain stated simply and patted Nevel on the back.

"Plans?" Nevel looked to the sea. The small boat was on its way back to shore. He looked at his Quinn. She was dying in his arms. He checked her pulse. It was so slow. He put the back of his sandy hand on her forehead. She had gone from hot to cold. He shook his head.

"Don't you see, Nevel?" the captain asked in a chilling whisper. "It's not just about information anymore. At first, it was. At first we all needed basic facts to remind us how to survive off the land, how to make things, how to grow food and care for animals." The captain continued to speak and Nevel knew it was important, but he couldn't concentrate. He couldn't take it in with Quinn dying in his arms. Nevel's eyes were on the men who were now approaching with a small wooden box of medicine. "But we're surviving now—we have been for some time," continued the captain. "It's not just about surviving anymore like it was in the dark ages of history. Now it's about becoming something more again. It's about the greatest species on earth—mankind. We must be more than just survivors if we are to thrive again. We must become more refined, more cultured. Don't you know your history, lad? Don't you remember what followed the dark ages?"

The first mate was back. He handed a small wooden box to the captain. The captain turned and handed it to Nevel. Inside were white antibiotic pills in a green glass bottle. With shaking hands, Nevel quickly grabbed the bottle and pulled the cork stopper out with his teeth, carefully pouring just one pill into his hand before re-corking the bottle. Quinn was out cold. He opened her mouth and pushed the pill into her throat, causing her to gag. He closed her mouth and held her jaw tight with his hands while she struggled wildly in panic and confusion. Soon he felt her neck accept the coarse pill and he released her, leaving her gasping for air. She immediately jolted a bit and took a long gasp of air into her lungs. Her eyes blinked furiously before closing again. But he knew her even breaths and color would begin returning slowly and steadily now. She would live! Nevel began to breathe again, wondering if he had taken even one breath in the last thirty minutes as he watched her die.

"I cannot thank you enough, Sir," Nevel said to the captain who was thumbing through the Register. He pulled out the two Passes of the Crow and handed them to Nevel.

"You keep these. Your pick-up will be in a week from the other side of that mountain." The captain pointed at the mountain that faced their lagoon and stood to go. Nevel tucked the Passes of the Crow in the waist of his pants. Quinn still wasn't lucid and continued to lie limp in Nevel's arms, but her color had returned some and her breathing had improved since the pill.

The captain turned to head to the ship. Still confused by what the captain had said, Nevel stroked Quinn's head and waited for the antibiotics to continue to bring her back to life.

Quinn's breathing was becoming more and more regular in his lap. "Thank you, Captain, thank you," was all Nevel could say as he watched him walk away.

Nevel watched as sailors loaded the small boats with crates of fruits and other island treasures. The tribal people watched as the sailors boarded the small boats. No one took notice of Branson's absence; it wasn't uncommon to leave a sailor behind. And the ship certainly wouldn't be lost without Quinn and Nevel's help. David waved at Nevel and Nevel waved back, grateful for his one friend on the ship.

As Nevel watched the Lilian Ruth sail away, he quietly retreated to the library in his mind. Pushing past the great mahogany door with its intricate carvings of Persephone and the changing of the seasons, he entered the place he had built mentally over a lifetime. His calloused hands ran along spines until he stopped at Walt Whitman and pulled it from the high shelf. He blew dust from its cover and carefully turned the thick crinkled pages until he reached what he had sought.

"O Captain my Captain! Our fearful trip is done,
The ship has weathered every rack, the prize we sought   is   won,
The port is near, the bells I hear, the people all exulting,
While follow eyes the steady keel, the vessel grim and daring..."

And the Lillian Ruth sailed away without them.

22

Encircled

Nevel felt alone, though he certainly was not. A line of tribal people, men and women and children with coffee-colored skin marked with white paint, lifted their knees and bent at the waist in a story-telling dance as they watched the ancient tall ship sail away. Every so often they turned away from the view of the ship to inspect Nevel and his limp Quinn. He knew they were wondering why these white folks had been left on the island. They chanted a song Nevel could not understand and, as the ship fell out of view, they began to draw their line from the sea's edge to where Nevel sat in the sand holding Quinn. The line encircled them and the song and dance continued. Nevel looked up, mystified. Were they welcoming them or wishing them away? Or were they chanting for Quinn's healing?

As the chant hummed in Nevel's ears, his mind finally began to accept and process what had happened over the course of the night and into this day. He replayed the events in his head and he felt like he was watching one of the old movies he remembered from childhood: Quinn had followed Nevel into the woods and watched him tie Branson to a tree. Quinn had slit Branson's throat and tried to wash away the evidence. Piranhas attacked her and her wound lay open for hours inviting infection. She would have died if Nevel hadn't found her and begged the captain for medicine. So Quinn would live, but she was a murderer. She was keeping secrets from Nevel. She wasn't who he thought she was. Nevel swallowed hard. He felt nauseous so he closed his eyes and took a long breath in an attempt to settle his mind. He opened his eyes again, feeling no better. With shaking hands, Nevel tucked the box with the medicine the captain had given him into the waist of his pants. Looking at Quinn in his lap made his queasiness worsen. The hypnotic dancers sang and moved around them still and he wished they would stop—the spinning, the spinning! His head and heart pounded with anxiety. He tried to retreat to the peacefulness of the library in his mind.

Focus on surviving, he told himself. *Follow protocol to meet the UBM's pick-up in a week. Deal with the girl later*, he told himself. He knew his books, his knowledge of the history of this place, could help him survive. Nevel tried to busy his mind by reading about the geography of Papua New Guinea, of volcanoes, typhoons, the ring of fire, but the tribal music beat too loudly in his ears and he lost focus. He turned to another book on the stories of the area and scanned over pages of plane crashes and missing persons who visited and were never seen again, but the chanting was still there and Quinn's body was shifting in his arms.

Suddenly his body was alive with nerves. He slid her head from his lap and onto the sand before jumping to his feet. The tribal song slowed and all eyes were on him. They continued their circle, slower and still crouching with watchful eyes, around Quinn who now lay alone on the sand and Nevel who stood with coursing blood. He wanted out. He turned and turned in a panic, looking for a break in the circle where he could run free. His mind spun with his body.

Why was he fighting for Quinn? She was a murderer! But how could he leave her? They had too much history together for him to give up now. The chanting drummed on. He had trusted her with everything. Nevel's hands were clamped in sweaty fists and he gritted his teeth. He was spinning. He loved her! He thought that she felt the same way, but now Nevel didn't know what to think. How could he be so naïve? He ran his fingers through his hair and wiped the sweat from his upper lip as his blood boiled. His confusion burned and twisted his stomach. He couldn't leave her with these natives. He had to keep giving her the antibiotics. He looked at Quinn lying in the sand, her red hair sprawled out like fire—like the fiery confusion that twisted inside him. He squeezed his eyes shut and when he opened them again, he burst out of the circle between two small children and ran and ran until his feet hit the water's edge.

Nevel dipped his hands in the cool water and splashed it against his face. *Get yourself together*, he told himself. His hands stung when the saltwater met them. They were covered in blisters and cuts from his arduous tasks aboard the ship pulling lines. He could not keep his mind from reliving the image of Branson's dead face. He looked out at the sea and took several deep breaths in until he felt his heart rate begin to slow from the rage on which it had been running. He looked at the mountain pick-up destination and reminded himself that he was an agent of the UBM and he still had work to do.

And then Nevel looked over his shoulder where he had left Quinn in a circle of natives in fear of what he might see. Two women were on their knees next to Quinn in the sand. They weren't harming her; Nevel could see that they were lifting her head gingerly, with care, as the chanting circle around them began to slow and then stopped altogether. One native woman was blotting her head with wet leaves; the other was spooning something into her mouth. They were nursing her back to health. She was clearly still passed out and Nevel felt guilty for leaving her side, but he also couldn't stand to be with her right now. The thought of her murdering Branson kept his stomach flipped upside-down, but the fact that she was a liar was tearing him apart inside. The islanders were helping her. He could take a moment to catch his breath.

Nevel's chest felt hot. He looked down to find the sun was scorching it into a blistered red mass. He had forgotten that he was shirtless. His shirt still dressed Quinn's ankle wound. He watched as the native women unwrapped it, ran to the water to dip the shirt in and ran back to her before re-wrapping it with palms and vines. The saltwater would help clean the wound. The palms and vines would help keep the sand and bugs out. He was confidant Quinn was in good hands. He was wary about what his next move would be.

Nevel looked to the other natives. They had gone back to their daily lives. One group of men worked to repair a roof on one of the huts. He watched as they stripped bamboo and laced vines and palms together before reinforcing the shelter. His eyes scanned to some children who were playing a game with shells. They were tossing beans back and forth between the shells and laughing. Closer to the water, a group of boys that couldn't have been much older than Nevel worked on some sort of fish trap: they braided strips of thin palm leaves with rapid hands until cone-shaped baskets emerged. Nevel took note of their method. It was genius. They repeatedly checked to make sure the insides of the traps were correct. At first, Nevel didn't know what they were looking at, but soon he realized that the leaves inside were forming sharp points that pointed in like arrows. Of course, he thought to himself, the fish could swim in but would have difficulty swimming back out. The boys, seemingly satisfied with their cone traps, went to the edge of the beach where the sand ended and the jungle floor began. They dropped to their knees and dug. Nevel assumed this would be the bait: bugs and worms. He was right. He watched them drop handfuls of wriggling insects into the bottoms of the traps before dropping the traps entirely underwater in the shallow edges of the sea.

Nevel moved his eyes to a small group of women working near what appeared to be a kitchen area based on all the small, contained fires and stacks of coconuts and palms. They stood at a table of sorts opening the thick fleshy stems of palm branches. He watched as they scraped and collected the fleshy bits. Nevel knew that heart of palm was a great source of calories and vitamins. It felt good to stop thinking about Quinn for a moment as he watched these natives thrive in their world that had always been void of technology.

Next the women took coconut after coconut and cracked them open on a sharp shell that protruded from a solid tree trunk table. Once open, they poured the liquid contents into a great wooden basin that had clearly been hollowed out of a tree trunk. Nevel watched them as they scraped the remaining coconut shells clean with a spear of bamboo, producing a pile of food on a wooden slab. The women then went to the water's edge and rinsed the husks, which were now bowls they filled with water. Nevel was amazed at their ingenuity.

In unison, the women poured their coconut bowls of seawater into a large wooden bowl that sat on the tree trunk table next to the piles of hearts of palm and coconut shavings. His stomach growled. Nevel watched as the women grabbed handfuls of small stones from a pile on the sand and dropped them into a fire pit. After a few minutes, one woman reached right into the fire with her hand wrapped in large leafy green palms that had been soaking in the saltwater, grabbed the rocks with this makeshift oven mitt, and dropped them quickly into the large seawater-filled wooden bowl. They then put a few small empty coconut bowls inside the bowl and covered it all with large, wet palm leaves. He had read about this before. Boiling saltwater would leave salt behind in the bowl that originally held the saltwater. The water would evaporate and drip from the leaf into the empty bowls, which would collect freshwater. He was amazed and delighted to see that the system did in fact work, but he knew it yielded an extremely small amount of water and was shocked at the patience of these people who worked so hard just for a bit of water. His own mouth was dry and his head ached.

The distraction of watching the island people had helped calm Nevel and he was ready to check on Quinn again. He walked over to where she still lay in the sand. The tribal women were fanning her with a large palm, but scattered when they saw Nevel approaching. His palms were sweaty and his mouth was dry. He sat on the sand next to her and looked at her. Even at death's door, she was beautiful. Even as a liar, a murderer, she held his heart. Nevel put the back of his sandy hand on her forehead. She was warm, maybe feverish. He had to move her to shade. He stood and scooped her up to move her to the shade beneath a palm he was eyeing at the edge of the jungle. He was surprised to see her open her eyes a bit.

"Don't..." she tried to speak, but her voice was

weak and she couldn't seem to muster up the energy needed to say what she wanted to say.

"I'm just moving you to the shade, Quinn," Nevel said without emotion.

"Leave me," she sputtered and her eyes closed again as her head fell onto his chest.

He didn't feel anything when she said it. He was numb. He walked the fifteen or so steps it took to get her beneath the shade of the palm tree and he laid her back down on the sand. One of her tribal caregivers appeared and handed Nevel a coconut bowl of fresh water and a palm leaf plate that contained coconut shavings.

"Thank you," he said, but he knew they couldn't understand and he knew that thank you was hardly enough for the amount of painstaking work these women had gone to in order to provide the bowl of fresh water.

Nevel sat on the sand next to Quinn and propped her head up in his lap. He quivered unknowingly when his skin touched hers. Lifting the bowl to her lips, he poured a bit of water in. Immediately it spilled out the corner of her mouth. Her eyes blinked open a few times before closing again.

"Quinn, you've got to drink this if you want to live," Nevel said robotically. This time she swallowed it. Next, he placed another antibiotic pill on her tongue and followed it with more water. Her eyes were still closed, but she seemed to swallow it. Nevel opened her mouth and looked inside to make sure it had gone down. He would try to give her three pills a day to rush her recovery.

"Good," he said. "I'm going to give you a bite to eat now." He fed her some coconut. It was thin enough that it dissolved on her tongue in small sheets, giving her at least a bit of sustenance.

"Don't," she whispered with a breathy voice. He ignored her and continued until he was satisfied enough was in her to keep the antibiotics from ripping her stomach to shreds and he watched as she drifted back into a restless sleep. The tribal women returned with more coconut shavings, heart of palm, and a husk of water. They pointed at Nevel. This round was for him. He nodded in thanks. His stomach was empty. The first bit of coconut to reach his lips was sweet and satisfying. He ate and drank and began to feel the exhaustion of the day's events catch up with him. Another rush of fever flashed over Quinn's body. He knew the antibiotics were fighting for her and was glad, or at least he thought he was glad. No, he knew he was. He had been faced with losing her forever and it had brought him to his knees. He couldn't lose her. He didn't want to. He would give her a chance to explain.

23

Survive

The sky turned pink and orange as the sun began its descent and Nevel looked to the natives who were busy in their lives. They now ignored Nevel and Quinn who still sat under a palm tree. He knew it was time to leave. They had done enough for them. He didn't want to overstay the welcome. He thought about giving one last thanks, but didn't know how or to whom and so he just stood, lifted Quinn, and walked away.

Nevel carried Quinn to their lagoon and placed her on the palette of palms he had built before everything had become so complicated. He lay down next to her and closed his eyes. He didn't remember much after that. He fell into a deep, drooling, hard sleep. He dreamt of empty gallows and New Government tattoos. He dreamt of a hooded executioner poking him in the ribs with a long wooden stick. He dreamt of Quinn's eyes rolling back in her head, choking on her breath. It jarred him awake. He sat up in a sweaty rush, surprised to see Quinn sitting by his side and looking back at him. The day was dawning. A choir of insects sung in the jungle behind them.

"Sorry, I didn't mean to startle you," she said. He looked at her and wondered if he was dreaming. She was alive. Nevel rubbed his eyes and looked again. This was no dream. "You're gonna have to fill me in. The last thing I remember is fish tickling my feet in the river." Quinn was quiet and weak. She scratched her messy head of hair and looked down at her wrapped ankle. Nevel thought about the time he found her outside the depository after his climb on the big rock. He had been sore and exhausted and she was full of spunk and chatter. This time was different. He felt the space between them. "I guess this is why I don't remember anything," she said looking down at her ankle and continuing without giving Nevel a chance to reply, "and why don't I see The Lilian Ruth?" she asked, looking at the sea.

"Just slow down, Quinn, you were really bad off," Nevel said. He was nervous. His heartbeat quickened. She didn't know how much he had learned. "You need to take it easy."

"Looks like you might need to take it easy too," she said eyeing his red, blistered chest.

It was good she was feeling better, but now Nevel knew he would have to face her. He felt sick thinking about the conversations they would have to have to-day. His stomach twisted thinking about Branson.

"The ship's gone." Nevel said, scratching his head and looking out at the water.

"What?!" Quinn tried to push herself up to stand, without any luck. She wavered and shook her head a bit as if her woozy mind snuck up on her.

"Careful, Quinn! You almost died!" Nevel warned as he pressed his hand against her back, helping her land softly back onto her seat on the palm bed.

"Wow, I am light-headed." Quinn used her arms to steady herself on the ground and then allowed her elbows to bend and slowly bring herself to lie down on her back. Flat on her back, Quinn took a deep breath before she continued to talk.

"It was that bad?" she asked.

"Yeah, you OK?" Nevel asked.

"Yeah, just seeing stars."

"It's gone," Nevel said matter-of-factly. "The ship's gone."

"Gone?" Quinn said as she swallowed hard the truth she was hearing, "What do you mean gone?" Quinn was clearly agitated at the news, but her body wouldn't allow her to physically respond with body language to match her mental state.

"How are we supposed to…What about the Register?" Quinn asked, trying to rub the stars out of her eyes.

"Gone with it." Nevel tossed a shell toward the sea nonchalantly. Quinn pushed herself up onto her palms, looking distraught.

"What do you mean?! That was our job! How

could you just…" Quinn looked at Nevel accusingly.

"The captain was UBM. He has it. It's safe," Nevel said and returned her accusatory look with a look of despair. "You were going to die, Quinn. Nothing else mattered. I would have given the Register, myself, whatever it took!"

Quinn looked away. She seemed conflicted. Nevel rolled his eyes. How could she be mad at him for saving her? Still, she seemed upset about the loss of the Register. She started picking at the shirt binding her wound.

"Sorry," she said softly. "Thanks, bookkeeper, I guess I owe ya." She was looking down nervously, moving her hands from fiddling with her bandage to poking holes in the sand with her fingers.

Nevel pulled her chin up with his forefinger to force her to meet his gaze. His heart dropped into his stomach. He had to ask. "Why were you in the jungle, Quinn?" he asked, but suddenly he found himself hoping she would lie because he wasn't ready for the truth.

"I was just looking for you, that's all." Her green eyes stared at him with conviction. Nevel was grateful for the lie, for now. They could save the truth for another day. *Tomorrow*, he told himself, *I'll make her confess tomorrow. I'll give her a day to regain her strength before I confront her with what I know.*

"Well, what do we do now?" she asked, tracing a circle in the sand with her finger.

"We do what we do best," Nevel said with a smile as he stood and looked out at the island before him. "Survive."

24

Waterfall

"I'm going to have to get moving to build strength in my leg," Quinn suggested from her palm bed.

"It's too soon." Nevel lay still next to her as she sat up, "You can't…"

"Build me some crutches or something. I know you've got a book in that head of yours with instructions on how to make me some crutches. I've got to get moving on this leg and build some stamina so I'm not just dead weight."

Dead weight. The words landed with a thud in Nevel's ears. She had been dead weight. He had carried her limp body. He knew she was right, though. She needed to figure out a way to survive leg and all, whether they moved on in this journey together or not. He didn't want her to be a sitting duck in the jungle. He moved to the edge of the jungle to begin to look for sturdy branches to make into crutches for Quinn.

Nevel sifted through a few limbs on the jungle floor until finding one that seemed sturdy enough. It was about twenty feet long and six inches wide. Nevel lifted it and tried to bend it over his knee. It didn't snap or curve; it passed the test. It was long enough that he could cut it to make two crutches of even size. Just before he reached for the knife in his shoe to get started, he looked at Quinn. She was busy doing something. He took a few inconspicuous steps closer to where she was for a clearer view. She was cutting her pants into shorts. *But the knife was in his shoe*, he thought to himself. He looked at her in confusion. She was holding a piece of clear glass the size of her hand, slicing away at the material. His heartbeat quickened.

"Oh, yeah," Quinn said when she caught him staring at it, "I brought it with me from the city. Found it on the street. I've had it flat against my back for days. It ought to come in handy, don'tcha think?"

Nevel just nodded and went back to working on the crutches, but he swallowed hard. He realized he could have just seen the murder weapon. Who was he kidding? He had just seen the murder weapon. He shook the thoughts from his head and went back to work. *Tomorrow*, he reminded himself, *tomorrow*.

After splitting the branch in two and measuring them to make sure they were equal in length, Nevel carved the top of the cut crutches into crooks where he wrapped leaves and twine in an attempt to leave a

147

soft spot for her armpits to rest. He soon finished the makeshift crutches and handed them to Quinn.

"You never cease to amaze me," Quinn smiled as she carefully pulled herself up and tried them out. "Not bad," she approved, but Nevel wasn't interested in her compliments. He watched her as she tottered back and forth on the sand as she gave them a try. "I think I'm steady enough. Care to join me for a walk?" she asked, looking toward the jungle with a smile that made Nevel feel irritated. Did she really believe she was getting off this easy?

Nevel shrugged and followed anyway. What else could he do? They penetrated the jungle slowly, Nevel making sure to register landmarks in his mind as they went so he would be able to find their way back home tonight.

"Hungry?" Nevel asked after a long while of walking in silence. He had stopped and was reaching his hand into a tree. They had wandered into an area of the jungle that teemed with fruit trees. Quinn grabbed a star fruit and started to eat.

"Delicious," she said. There was an awkwardness between them.

Nevel held a mango and sunk his teeth in. His mouth exploded with sweet sugary nectar. It was divine. Monkeys swung in a banana tree. Colorful birds swooped in and out of the lush green canopy above. Chirping and buzzing sounds made jungle music in unison. Tiny green frogs hopped on fallen mossy logs. Water dripped from vines and Nevel and Quinn both dropped their open mouths beneath for a taste. For a moment, Nevel forgot it all—the lies, the worries—

and just marveled at his surroundings. He reached for a bunch of bananas. Quinn tossed him a star fruit and he returned the favor with a mango. They both stuffed what they could in their waistbands to save for later. Nevel bit into the star fruit and thought his mouth would explode from the rush of citrus that brought his taste buds to life.

"This place is amazing. I haven't eaten anything like this ever in my life, I don't think." Quinn wiped her mouth on the shoulder of her shirt. "I swear fruit didn't even taste this good from the stores before the MegaCrash," Quinn said, still devouring the fruit and leaning on the crutches. She smiled and pointed at creatures in the tree.

"Tree Kangaroos," Nevel explained and smiled too as he watched them. He then began identifying all the creatures he saw with a book in his mind on jungle life.

"Ornithoptera Alexandre," Nevel said pointing at a butterfly with aqua and black wings that looked as if they had been hand-painted.

"Frilled lizard," Nevel pointed to a small brown lizard about the size of a kitten that stood a few feet from Quinn. He smiled as Quinn's eyes widened. The lizard looked like a species from prehistoric dinosaur times. It scampered its brown body across the jungle floor with confidence and stopped just short of Quinn, fanning out the pleated skin around its face. Quinn jumped back and it ran away. Nevel couldn't help but laugh.

"Why did it do that?" Quinn asked.

"Showing off for you, I guess," Nevel explained

before pointing out another creature that stirred near Quinn.

"New Guinean Rat," he identified as a long tail slipped away under a bush.

"Eww," Quinn said, moving closer to Nevel and further from the rat's place of escape.

"Shall we keep moving?" she asked. "I think I'm all caught up on the jungle creatures for now."

Nevel smiled and nodded as they turned to move on through the jungle. Quinn was managing just fine with the crutches, considering they were homemade and she was moving over pretty rough terrain.

"Wonder how long it would take us to reach that volcano," Quinn called to Nevel who hiked behind her.

"You're crazy, Quinn." Nevel laughed and ignored her request. He looked to the sky and pointed at the plume of smoke that was rising in the distance. "This is as close as I'll let you get!"

They came to a beautiful waterfall that was surrounded by lush ferns covering the ground and a rocky wall built right into the island.

"No swimming today," Nevel warned and pointed to Quinn's ankle.

"Have you ever seen anything like it?" Quinn said in awe.

"Only in the books in my mind," Nevel replied.

A mossy rock jutted out near the waterfall and Nevel went and sat on it. Quinn followed suit, propping her injured ankle up on a fallen log.

"How's it feel?" Nevel asked, looking at her ankle, knowing she should be resting instead of exploring a jungle on it.

"Not bad, I'll suffer through," Quinn said and bit into a mango before offering a bite to Nevel.

They were in paradise. They had spent the day collecting fruits and exploring the wilds of an island that Nevel never imagined he would see in real life. Still, so much remained unanswered and Nevel knew the time was coming that he would have to ask questions. Even knowing she was a liar and a murderer, he wanted to kiss her sitting on that rock, but the air was thick between them now. Secrets swallowed the trust they had before. Nevel wasn't ready to go back to how things were until he knew more. Today he just wanted to enjoy the island. Today wasn't the day for answers.

"Nevel," Quinn's voice broke his wandering thoughts and caught his attention, "this has been good. My leg is getting stronger. I know I can move on it at least, but we can't just explore the island forever, can we? We've got work to do, right?"

"We'll be OK until…"

"Until what?"

"Sorry, I never finished filling you in," Nevel replied honestly, "The captain said the UBM had other plans for me. Who knows what those are? He said my pick-up would be in a week on the other side of the mountain that faces our lagoon."

"*Your* pick-up?" Quinn's wide eyes blinked as she looked at Nevel.

"Well, us, I guess; you were dying, remember?" Nevel reassured.

"How are we going to get there? What kind of

pick-up will it be?" Quinn demanded, wringing her hands.

"I don't know, but he made sure we still had the Passes of the Crow, which I have right here," Nevel said as he patted at his waist where they were tucked in his pants and reviewed what the captain had said in his mind. "The only other thing he said was something about it not just being about survival anymore."

"You mean like what the invisible message said in the register?" Quinn met his stare.

Nevel couldn't believe he hadn't put the pieces together. "Of course, yes. *Let us exhume the culture of our past.*"

"So, somehow, this is our new mission?" Quinn wondered aloud. Nevel stood and offered a hand to help pull her up. She was right, they were better as a team.

"I just don't know. The only thing I know for sure is I think it's time we get back to our lagoon," Nevel said. "You've been on your leg enough today."

"Righty-oh," Quinn said and the two began to re-trace their steps through the jungle towards their makeshift island home.

Back at the lagoon, Nevel decided to try his luck at spear fishing. The fruit was amazing, but he was hungry for meat. He also wanted to get out a bit of aggression. He grabbed the bamboo spear he had sharpened as Quinn had been rehabilitating.

"I…" Quinn started.

"You need to stay put and rest," Nevel said dis-missively as he pulled the passes of the crow from his pants and dropped them on the palm bed before grabbing the spear and taking off toward the clear, blue water.

Nevel waded in waist-deep water, with his spear held tight in his right fist. His eyes scanned the water. There were plenty of fish. Shouldn't be too hard, he thought. A large blue fish with black stripes swam by and Nevel thrust his spear at it only to watch it easily swim away. This was how it went. Again and again, Nevel stalked and stabbed at fish that seemed to be just in his reach, but every time they easily escaped. Nevel's frustration grew with each miss. The fish were right in front of him, but they were completely unattainable.

Hours passed. Nevel wasn't giving up. The un-yielding sun beat down on his bare skin and scorched his shoulders. He didn't care. He knew it would be gone soon as night quickly approached. He glanced up at the beach and saw Quinn working on lighting a fire. He returned his attention to the fishing. The more he missed, the hungrier he became and the more deter-mined he was not to leave the water without a fish.

Finally, a parrotfish circled the area just in front of him. Nevel held his breath and reached his arm way back. In one swift motion, his arm shot forward like an arrow from a bow and he sent the spear sliding straight through the side of the fish. Elated, Nevel lifted his spear from the sea and held it high above his head in victory.

Quinn waved her approval from the sand and Nevel's elation turned back into anger. Nevel's frus-tration at the fruitless hours he had spent fishing cou-pled with the adrenaline he felt upon catching the rainbow fish bubbled over until he felt a blinding rage at Quinn and her lies. Who was she really?

25
The Truth

Nevel held his catch over the fire to cook and sat silently in his wet pants as he watched the flames. The sun was setting, but Nevel's mind was alive. Branson's wide-eyed dead face flashed across his mind over and over again as he stared at the fire.

"Great catch!" Quinn lightheartedly congratulated Nevel, but he did not respond.

"What is it?" Quinn asked, concerned.

Nevel's eyes were narrow and his expression was harsh and unforgiving. His anger had finally caught up with him. He couldn't sit another second without knowing. "You killed him," Nevel said. "You killed him. I saw you there." He spoke without ever looking at her; his eyes were on the flames.

Quinn turned and faced him. The dark was creeping in. A strange, cold wind whipped in out of nowhere. Chills ran across Nevel's body. Only her eyes showed as she spoke. "You didn't see me. You're confused," Quinn said, but her voice sounded different. She didn't sound offended at his accusation. She sounded as if she was telling him what he should believe. She looked like the old Quinn, the one who had held him captive in the outback. The wind howled and whipped faster and colder; the tropical island began to feel very different.

"Why did you kill him? I had taken care of it. He was tied to the tree. He couldn't..." Nevel's palms were sweaty and his heart was racing. He felt scared of her again. He hadn't felt that way in months. A cold wind began to swoop in and Nevel's arms flushed with shivers.

"I had to, OK!" Quinn shouted in admission as she slammed her fist on the bed of palms, "He was going to hurt me!"

"How?" Nevel demanded. "He was tied to a bloody tree in the middle of a jungle! You went after him! You're lying!"

Quinn grabbed the crutches that lay next to her and stood up. When she was balanced, she kicked the sand with her good foot. Nevel stood and grabbed her right bicep to turn her towards him. She wobbled and then shook him off and took off hobbling toward the water.

"What have you got to hide?" Nevel chased after her, screaming. "What did Branson know about you that I don't?"

At the water's edge, under the light of the moon, Quinn turned to Nevel and her eyes were filled with tears. The cold wind slapped Nevel across the face and he could feel his skin sting. Something icy and wet fell on his nose. He brushed it away. Another fell on his upper left eyebrow. He brushed it away too. It wasn't until the third and fourth and fifth drops that he paid them any mind.

"What is this?" Nevel looked up and held his palms out, facing the sky as if to question the clouds themselves. Quinn was looking up too and then down at the precipitation falling softly on her forearms.

"I think it's snow!" Quinn said, clearly baffled as she rubbed her arms while leaning her weight on the crutches. She shivered.

"Unbelievable," Nevel said as he turned in circles catching snowflakes on his hands and tongue and face. It was the MegaCrash. It could change the weather on a dime, but never had Nevel seen it snow. His mind spun to frosted evergreen trees, snowmen, and sleds—things he had only ever read about. He didn't expect to see his first snow on a tropical island as he confronted the girl he loved about murder. He snapped himself back into the moment.

The snow had gone as quickly as it had arrived. The winds changed back from cold to warm. The water slowly lapped their feet.

"If I tell you, bookkeeper, I may lose you forever and you're all I've got."

Nevel was scared to know the truth, but he had to find out what it all meant. "We're in this together, Quinn! We can't have any secrets! I have trusted you with my life!"

"And I've trusted you with mine, Nevel!" she cried and now sobs wracked her body. "You don't know everything! OK? You don't *have* to know everything! Some things are just better left unsaid!"

Nevel was shaking. His heart was beating out of his chest. "What is so important that I don't know about you that's worth killing a man over? What is so important that you risked your own life to cover it up?" Nevel shouted at her, enraged. She was standing in his storm, taking every blast without letting any knock her down. He felt betrayed and alone. "Why can't I know? What could possibly be so bad that you would have to keep it from me?"

Nevel was inches from her face. She opened her lips to speak, but she did not shout like he did. Her words were carried on whispers. "I...worked...for...the...government." A single tear slid down her face.

Nevel took a step backward in the wet sand. His heart sank. He continued stepping backwards into the dark, all the while she held his gaze steadily.

How could he not know her? How could he have come this far with a stranger? An enemy?

"I...I don't anymore...it was before..." she pleaded calling out to him as he continued backing away from her until he disappeared into the night.

26
Native

Nevel turned and ran down the beach towards the small village where the Lillian Ruth had made trades. He ran toward the bonfire and the sounds of island drums. He didn't know what he was doing. He just knew he had to get away from Quinn. He had to clear his head. He had to rethink his plan. He was alone now. This was how it would be from now on.

His feet pushed forward, step after jogging step, but his mind remained stuck: Quinn worked for the government. Nevel felt as if he would be sick as his stomach churned with disgust and betrayal. Had this all been a ruse? Had Quinn chased him into the outback months ago not as a girl in search of her parents, but as a government spy? Had she befriended him,

159

made him fall in love with her, just to gather intelligence on the Underground Book Movement? How could he ever believe a word she said? Nevel's feet rushed forward at a faster pace as the questions in his mind quickened. He ran away from her, from the questions spinning in his head, as fast as he could.

The bonfire of the tribal village in the distance grew closer and closer. Nevel's breaths were short and choppy, his chest throbbed as his arms pumped up and down. His face was wet; he didn't bother to determine if it was from sweat or tears. Sounds of villagers grew louder until he was almost in the middle of them. Nevel stopped at the edge of the tiny village and observed from the dark night's cover.

Men who danced around the fire wore animal hides and leaf flaps to conceal their manhood and were bare-chested like Nevel. Topless women wore grass skirts; many were dancing while others were cooking, tending bowls and skewers over a smaller fire. Children were naked, dancing around the adults or playing and splashing at the water's edge. All of the tribal people wore shells on necklaces and bracelets tied around their legs and ankles. The shells made beautiful sounds when they clinked together. Many of the people had animal bones through their noses and ears. They chanted and danced and struck their drums to a tribal beat that matched the shaking of the shells they wore.

Nevel walked in a trancelike state to the gathering of natives near the bonfire. Nevel stood out in the group, a white boy in tattered shorts, seemingly discarded by the ship that had delivered him here, but he didn't care. Nevel couldn't speak their language. He assumed the crew of the Lilian Ruth couldn't either. Nevel knew from the books in his mind that this island had over eight hundred tribes and over eight hundred languages. He knew enough to take comfort in the fact that these were a friendly people as they had already welcomed his old crew and helped nurse Quinn back to life. Perhaps he would stay with them until he figured out what to do.

The natives looked at Nevel strangely. Many stopped their banter and stared. Others walked around him, looking him up and down and calling out words Nevel didn't understand. Surely they knew who he was, Nevel thought. They had watched the events unfold when the captain demanded medicine be retrieved for a dying Quinn on the beach. They had witnessed the Lilian Ruth's departure, while Nevel and Quinn were left behind. To them, Nevel assumed, he was the castaway. Nevel couldn't expect these people would be happy about his presence now; he was a stranger in their territory. Nevel didn't care if he was welcomed or endangered. His heart was broken. His mind was spinning.

While the sounds came from many of the tribal people, Nevel began to notice where the main source of the music was derived. Three men sat on tree stumps at the end of the bonfire. Each held bongo-type drums that they slapped with the palms of their hands in rhythmic beats. A young boy stood by them with sticks that were covered in hollowed shells and he shook them to the drumbeats, producing a sound that was melodic and began to invade the hollow cavern of Nevel's chest. Nevel began to shake his head in pace with the beat. A few of the women opened their mouths and began lifting their voices to the sky in tempo with the instruments.

Nevel began to clap his hands to the music and let his feet mimic the dancing feet of those around him. The dancing tribal people all joined in and the song turned into more of a chant now that Nevel danced. Nevel continued to clap and move his feet on the sand, spinning in circles to the drums and keeping pace with the chant. He realized his eyes had been closed for a few moments and so he opened them and took in the shadows produced by the dancing flames and tribal people. Soon he realized that he wasn't dancing with them, but surrounded by them. The circle that had surrounded the bonfire now encompassed Nevel. The chanting grew louder and louder and he let go more and more and danced wildly, forgetting about it all. He wasn't Nevel. He wasn't a bookkeeper. He wasn't an agent of the UBM. He wasn't the boy who loved the enemy. He let go of the world and let the island take hold.

27

Sage

Nevel awoke on a straw mat under a thatched roof. Smoke billowed through a hole in the ceiling of the hut. It smelled of sage. Nevel had read once that sage was burned to rid places of evil spirits. He wondered if the tribal people who had taken him in were cleansing the air to protect themselves from him.

He looked down at himself. His skin was pink and tan and leathery from the sun and salt of the last few days. He reached to scratch his head. His locks were knotted in chunks of hair that had twisted in the island wind and water. He looked around the room. A small islander in a grass skirt with long braided hair was squatting on the ground a few feet away, watching him and quietly humming a chant while mixing something in a bowl. She was the only other person in the room. She was older; her skin was wrinkled and stretched and her hair showed streaks of grey. She was thin and very involved in her task.

Nevel didn't know if he was a captive or a guest. He remembered dancing long into the night amid the chants and tribal drums. He must have fallen asleep at some point and someone must have taken him into this hut to rest, or to be kept captive. Nevel was not afraid. He had known far greater threats than this and he no longer even knew what he was living for, so he simply lay on the mat and waited for whatever would come next.

The tribal lady crawled to him like a preying panther, bowl in hand. When she was inches from his face, she held the bowl to his lips and said something in a language he did not know. Nevel obliged and drank. The concoction was bland and meaty, like oatmeal but with animal fat of some sort. It was slick on his tongue and fell down his throat before he even had a chance to swallow. It could be poison or remedy; he would find out soon enough. Nevel didn't care either way.

The woman stayed near him, squatting like a cat and watching. Nevel could feel a rush course through his veins. He felt alive, replenished, and he sat upright. The woman backed up and motioned with her waving hand at the door, as if to shoo away a pest. Nevel stood too quickly and fell back down on the mat. Rubbing his eyes and trying again, Nevel sat up slowly and then pushed himself to stand. She shooed him again and he slowly walked to the door to exit the hut. He nodded to the woman in thanks and she shooed him again. He exited, realizing now that he had indeed been a guest and not a prisoner.

The morning sun outside was bright. Rows of boats, canoes carved or burned from trees, carried rowing tribal people across the water. They seemed to be fishing as they dipped sticks and baskets into the water. The woman followed Nevel out of the hut and again made the shooing motion with her waving hand. Nevel pointed at the boats.

"I can help." He pointed at himself in the chest with his thumb and pointed out at the boats again. "I can fish."

The woman said something unknown back, shaking her head and continuing to shoo him away toward the lagoon from which he came.

Nevel took the hint. It was time for him to go, but where?

He looked at the mountain the captain had pointed out to him. He could go now, without her. He could jump in a boat with one of these village fishermen and be ferried across the water right now. He could leave her here on the island and never see her again. The pick-up would be in a few days. And then Nevel remembered the Passes of the Crow. They were still at the lagoon. He may not be picked up without them; the captain made sure they were in his possession.

He looked down the beach at the lagoon. She was there; he knew she was. Where else would she go? Last night he couldn't face her, but soon enough he would have to. He couldn't help but love her still, yet he had so many questions: Had she been against him all along? Was her traveling with him a part of a bigger government scheme? She was the only person in the world he thought he could trust, and she was still a stranger to him.

Nevel began walking toward the lagoon. He would have to face her. He had not yet decided whether she would be with him when he left for that mountain for pick-up. She was right. He didn't know everything and there were no books in his head that could explain all of this. He would have to go to her for answers, whether he liked it or not.

28

Return

Nevel arrived at the lagoon to find Quinn swimming, her crutches lying useless on the beach. She was beautiful as always. Her hair was growing back and was past her ears now and she had unwrapped the binding from her chest. She gracefully dipped in and out of the waves in her white shorts and shirt, unaware of his return. Nevel went to the palm leaf mat where his bloodstained shirt that had wrapped her ankle hung to dry in the sun. He sat on the bed of palms and watched her, trying to think of what he would say and wondering if anything she had ever told him had been the truth. His blood boiled. His heart rushed.

Finally, Quinn noticed him sitting there and, seemingly embarrassed at her lack of concentration, quickly swam ashore. Walking from the waves, her limp was still evident and he couldn't help but want to help her, but he stood his ground. She stopped where the waves were breaking and wrung out her hair and shirt before slowly walking past the crutches and towards Nevel. Nevel sat with his arms wrapped around his bent knees and stared right past her out at the blue sea.

"I'm glad you came back," she said in a soft voice.

Nevel rolled his eyes.

"There's a lot we need to talk about," she said as she sat next to him on the sand, but not too near so as to give him his space.

"You think?" Nevel replied sarcastically.

"Just listen to what I have to say, Nevel. I promise it is not as bad as you think." Quinn took a deep breath as if to summon courage from the base of her lungs.

"And why should I believe one word that falls from your lips?" Nevel turned and looked at Quinn with disgust, disgust at her…disgust at himself for being so naïve.

"I have nothing left to hide, Nevel. This was it. I never wanted you to know, but now that you do, I have no reason to lie anymore."

Nevel stood up and kicked the sand before turning to Quinn who was still sitting and nervously twisting her shirt to wring out water.

"You have been lying to me since the day we first spoke! I don't even know who you are!" Nevel's voice was shaky. He was lost. His heart ached.

Quinn slowly pushed herself off the sand to stand. She placed more weight on her good ankle while she rested on the tiptoes of her injured ankle. He figured she had stopped using the crutches now, as they still lay useless in the sand. Nevel looked down and saw the wound was starting to close itself and heal, but he couldn't help but wonder if she was still taking the antibiotics and keeping the ankle wrapped on land. He hit himself in the forehead with the palm of his right hand; why did he care?

"Nevel, I used to work for the government some. That's why I knew Branson and that's why he knew me. But it was long before any of this." Quinn stumbled a bit and Nevel turned to catch her.

"Just sit, you'll break your other bloody ankle." Nevel rolled his eyes and sat again, this time on the sand closer to Quinn.

"I was twelve or thirteen when I started my trips into the outback to hunt on the weekends. You remember me telling you about that, about how my father and brothers could have cared less where I was." Quinn spoke slowly and steadily, waiting for Nevel's nod before continuing.

"I was mad at the world, mad at my mother for dying, mad at my father for pretty much dying with her, mad at my brothers for their bloody entitled attitudes." Quinn crossed her legs and put her head in her hands and continued speaking with her head hung in shame.

"I was the smartest one in all of my classes. The government always paid attention to that." She looked at Nevel who wouldn't look her in the face and she continued. "After sitting in on my classes for a couple weeks, they tested me to make sure I wasn't a book-keeper."

"You had already been tested?" Nevel stood up, enraged. He pulled at the locks on his head with both hands until it hurt. His teeth were clenched and his muscles were tense. He puffed air out of his cheeks to try to control the anger that boiled up from his gut. "Did they even test you again before the trial? When we were in jail?" Nevel paced back and forth scratching his head and yelling the questions into the air. "Or were you just sitting in the back drinking coffee with the boys and faking your injuries to put on a show?" Nevel was trying to put all the pieces together, but each question in his head led to another and his anger grew stronger with each. "Were you even on trial or was it all just a scam?"

Quinn stood to face him, but wobbled before giving up and sitting back down. She pleaded her case from the sand, looking up at the ever-moving Nevel, but never catching his eye. "The jail, the questioning, the trial...it was all real! They knew I had been tested before, but they worried I had outsmarted them before. They thought maybe they had missed something. I was on trial just like you! It was all real!"

Nevel took a deep breath, not knowing what to believe. Still, he didn't understand how she had worked for the government. He didn't know how she could have kept all of this a secret. He had just saved her life and he didn't know if she was the enemy or not! Again! How could he fall for her again despite all that she had lied to him about?

Quinn must have sensed that Nevel was letting his mind fill with even more questions that he was not sharing aloud and so she continued. "After I failed the testing years ago, I was approached about data running." Quinn's voice was soft, subdued, and her body language was akin to a dog with its tail tucked between its legs.

Nevel looked at her for a moment and then rolled his eyes and shook his head. *How could she?* was all he could think. "What the hell does that mean?" Nevel asked disinterestedly as he turned to face the water, still too disgusted to even look at her.

"They wanted me to spy, gather info, turn it in to the government." Quinn kept her head low. "They said I was obviously smart and so I could do big things for the government. I felt important for the first time. I was getting attention. The bloke who set me up was one of Carrington's aids. His name was Russell. He told me he would get me things if I kept him informed on the families in town."

"What kind of things?" Nevel's voice oozed irritation.

"Clothes, boots..." Nevel thought of her pink snakeskin boots with metal tips. A fire raged in his heart. He had hated them when he saw her in them in school because he knew she was pretentious. Now he hated them even more.

"So, you told them about my family? Me? The UBM?" Nevel felt he would explode at the thought of Quinn spying on him for years.

"NO!" She lifted her head and tears were falling, "I never told them anything about you or your family!

I really didn't know about the UBM or your family!"

"Why should I believe you? Did information about me buy you those pretty little boots?" Nevel chucked a seashell from the sand almost to the water's edge.

"No! I only told them bits and pieces about stupid little things—who was talking bad about the government, who had the best food plots, who knew how to successfully breed animals. It was never enough and so they dropped me after only a few months. They dropped me before I ever even knew who you were!" Quinn sounded desperate for Nevel to believe her, but he wasn't biting yet. "Branson was another data runner just like me. I saw him once or twice when we would meet to offer our info."

"Why should I believe you?" Nevel turned to her and looked her straight in the eye.

"I don't know, Nevel. That's why I had to kill Branson. I knew you wouldn't believe me if you ever found out." Quinn eyes pleaded with Nevel. "This was years before I even realized who you were. None of it matters. Everything between us has been real. I have not lied to you about anything else."

Nevel reached down and picked up another shell and threw it just a hard as he could to the water where it skipped at least four times before slowly disappearing beneath the surface. A familiar feeling crept back into Nevel's heart, one that been there before this whole crazy adventure with Quinn had ever begun, one he had been glad to be rid of until now; loneliness. He was alone again, standing right next to the girl he loved. His whole life, Nevel had always had all the answers...until now.

29

Letting Go

Quinn remained sitting in the sand with her head hanging low between her knees. Nevel could hear the sobs. They seemed sincere, but maybe it was all a game to her. His heart was telling him to forgive her and forget it all and his mind was telling him to refocus and figure out a plan.

But his mind was foggy and he felt he would pass out or be sick. Nevel lay down on the bed of palms placing his right arm across his face to shield his eyes from the sun. He could hear her coming toward him, but he did not uncover his eyes. They stung and were watery. His breaths were as rapid as his heartbeat.

He felt Quinn lay down next to him, though she didn't dare touch him and he didn't dare move. And then she whispered to him, "I'm sorry I didn't tell you, Nevel, but I'm all in. I always have been. No more secrets, I promise."

Nevel let the words fill his ears and soak into his soul. He tried to slow his breathing to a place where he could let go. His thoughts began to race with doubt again, but he was tired of feeling angry. He thought of the tribal drums from the night before and he replayed the chanting in his mind while his slowing heartbeat played out the rhythm. He let go. He let go.

Nevel's arms were wrapped around his Quinn when he awoke on the bed of palms. She was fast asleep and he worried if he let her go, she would awake and realize that he had been holding her. Still, if he stayed she would find out all the same. Nevel began to pull at his left arm, which lay below her sleeping body. Immediately, she turned to him and opened her eyes inches from his face from within the crook of his arm.

Nevel thought he felt his heart stop. He wanted to kiss her. He could feel the heat of her breath against his lips. He pulled away quickly and sat up. Not again, he warned himself.

Quinn sat up too and looked at him again, still too close for Nevel's comfort.

"Today, we make our new plan," Nevel said in a serious tone and he swore he saw Quinn grin from ear to ear as she pushed herself up to stand. Of course she's happy, Nevel thought, she was getting away with murder.

"Deal," she said, and she headed to the water.

Nevel followed her. He was hot from his night's

rest and the water looked so inviting. Without speaking, they both waded in and began to cool their sticky skin by dousing themselves with the cool, blue waves. Nevel kept his distance from Quinn and she seemed to be trying to respect his position, happy not to be completely cast off yet.

Nevel looked out across the water at the green, lush mountain, which stood across from their lagoon. Nevel cupped his hands over his eyes and really took it in.

"Whatcha thinkin', bookkeeper?" Quinn asked.

Nevel didn't feel the same now when she called him by this name. He wasn't captivated by her flirtation. He was remaining guarded. "I'm thinking about how we are going to get to that mountain." Nevel was all business.

"It's not that far, but too far to swim," Quinn said, also cupping her hands over her eyes to see.

"Today, we build a boat." Nevel said before dipping his head once under water and then heading back to shore with Quinn following behind.

On shore, they both shook the water off like dogs. Quinn reached in the crook of a nearby tree and tossed Nevel a mango and a star fruit.

"I gathered them yesterday," was all she said as she bit into a mango herself. Nevel nodded, forced a "thanks," and took a bite of the island fruit. It was still very easy for Nevel to be swept away by the intense flavors of the fruit here; they were nothing like anything he had ever tasted before. After losing himself in his satisfying breakfast, Nevel regrouped and started looking at the jungle in search of a tree trunk that might suffice as a boat. He hadn't figured out yet exactly how he would cut down and get a tree trunk to their lagoon, but he had a great book in his mind called *The Great Skills of Native Americans* that showed him step-by-step how to hollow out a tree with fire in order to make a canoe.

"We've got to find a large tree trunk and drag it to shore." Nevel motioned with his hand for Quinn to follow him into the jungle. They marched over fallen dead trees and ferns and vines. Nothing looked promising. As he walked, he read the book in his mind and realized just how lengthy and painstaking the process would be. Then he remembered the boats he had seen the natives in and he wondered how he could persuade them to share. They had nothing to trade, no junky gadgets. His only tradable item was knowledge, and yet they did not speak the same language.

"What's going on in that mind of yours, Nevel?" Quinn asked as they walked aimlessly through the middle of a dense jungle in silence.

"Sorry, I was lost in thought," he said.

"Clearly," Quinn said sarcastically and Nevel rolled his eyes. He wasn't ready for their usual banter. She wasn't yet forgiven. He didn't know if she ever would be. His mind left the book on Native American skills and began again to fill with questions about Quinn and her recent confession about having worked for the government.

"So did you speak to Chief Commander Carrington during your stint with the government?" Nevel asked with a harsh, condemning tone.

"No, I never even saw him," Quinn replied as they

walked on over vines and slippery groundcover.

"Where did you meet...what was his name again, Russell?"

"Russell was one of those suits who would often sit in the backs of the classrooms, keeping watch, taking notes. You probably even saw him. He stopped me after school one day and told me he was taking me in for questioning." Quinn spoke clearly as she followed Nevel through the jungle. She seemed to be willing to divulge as many details as it would take to re-earn his trust. "That was when they tried to see if I was a bookkeeper. They weren't rough with me then like they were with us at the jail. I willingly followed him to Government Square into the brick building next to the courthouse." Quinn looked to him as if to ask him if he remembered that particular building, but Nevel was looking at the trail. She went on. "He offered me tea and I sat in a room with lavish furniture, rugs, and paintings and I answered questions, or at least I tried to." Quinn stumbled a bit, stepping down perhaps a bit too hard on her bad ankle and had to catch herself with a vine. Nevel peered over his shoulder nonchalantly to see she was ok, but quickly continued marching without coming to her aid. She took a breath and went on. "When they were convinced that I was not a bookkeeper, just a smart kid, they let me go. Then, a few days later the same guy, Russell, was outside of school waiting for me. He invited me back for tea. I went. He offered me the opportunity to do some information gathering, data running was what he called it." Nevel was coming to an area that sloped downward. He knew Quinn would struggle with the slippery floor of the rainforest and so, without looking at her, he stopped and dutifully offered his hand. She smiled and took it, trying to catch his eye, but as soon as she made it down the stretch he quickly let go and moved on. "He told me it was for a census they were doing. They needed accurate accounts of how many people were in households, how many and what kinds of animals they had, how many and what kinds of food plots they had, how many and what kinds of personal items they had. They told me I would have to do this in secret in order to get accurate accounts. And in order to get my reward."

"You were inventory." Nevel said, unamused at her being a traitor to his countrymen. He knew the government would commandeer livestock, crops, furnishings, and other goods from his neighbors and the people of town, calling them "taxes." Quinn had just told them who had what so they wouldn't have to do their own research before their reaping.

"I know, Nevel, now. I didn't think it was wrong at the time. I didn't think I was hurting anyone. I was a kid." Nevel didn't know if it was all the talking or if her leg was really giving her a hard time, but Quinn was getting really out of breath. Nevel felt bad, for just a fleeting moment, for dragging her into the jungle and drilling her on her involvement with the government. And then he thought again about the task at hand, coming out of the jungle with a tree trunk to turn into a boat...with a hobbling breathless girl who had nearly died days before and he realized the ridiculousness of it all. Who was he kidding?

"Never mind this. Let's head back."

"Head back? Without our tree?" Nevel knew the old Quinn would have made a sarcastic comment about what a waste of time this journey had been, but she seemed to be trying to remain on her best behavior since her secret had crept out.

"The natives on the shore that the Lilian Ruth traded with—they have boats," Nevel said as he trekked back through the jungle towards the beach.

"What makes you think they will let us borrow one?" Quinn asked, swatting a spider web from her face and still walking with a limp despite the improvement in her ankle.

"I'm thinking about that," Nevel said and then looked down at her foot and asked, "You're still taking the antibiotics, right?"

"Yes, sir!" Quinn replied with a smile.

It was impossible to stay mad at her long.

Nevel thought about what he could offer to the tribal people. He was glad he didn't have junk to trade because he didn't want to trick them, undermine them, treat them as less than himself. Still, what could he offer? The books in his mind did no good if they didn't speak the same language. He couldn't teach them about survival; they were the experts. He was in awe of their success despite the MegaCrash. It hadn't fazed them. They had never relied on technology like the rest of the world. They survived before and they survived after.

"Nevel," Quinn broke the silence as they neared the beach.

"Yeah," he said, still deep in thought about how to

barter for a boat.

"I wanted to tell you something." Quinn was behind him and so Nevel stopped and turned around to find her limping up to him, biting her lower lip and looking doe-eyed.

"What is it?" he asked, still not completely himself around her.

She took his hand. He started to pull back, but she squeezed it and wouldn't let go. "Just listen and don't say anything back. I have to say something and I don't want you to reply, got it?" He looked at her and she looked him in the eyes. "I fell in love with you in the outback." Nevel kicked at the ground, looking at his feet. She continued, "Somewhere between me chasing you and us climbing up the face of that rock. Or maybe it was just before we were taken by Driscoll's men or even in your house when you were saying goodbye to your parents. I don't know, but somewhere along this crazy journey I fell in love with you."

She was still holding his hand. He looked down. He couldn't look her in the eyes.

"How do you even know? We're young. Maybe it's just..." Nevel tried to downplay it, not knowing how to respond to the girl who he loved, feared, and hated all at the same time. He kicked at the ground.

"I do know, Nevel." He finally looked up at her as she continued, "We're just like Mr. Darcy and Lizzie. We have hated each other, yes, but we can't deny how that changed somewhere along the way." Nevel looked at his feet again. He didn't know what to say. She kept on, "I know you don't trust me again yet.

You don't have to say it to me. I don't want you to say it yet." She laced her fingers through his before letting go of his hand, "I know you haven't completely forgiven me yet, maybe you never will. But I had to tell you because whatever happens from this point forward, I need you to know that I love you. I love you, Nevel."

Nevel felt his stomach turn and his mouth go dry. He was at a loss for words. He tried to open his mouth but there were no words. Quinn kissed him on the cheek and hobbled past him to the beach.

His mind spun to the redhead showing up at his front door unannounced, to their brawl in his home. He saw her chasing him from a distance in the wild of the outback. He saw her across the crackling fire in the desert, in the depository deep in her book. He saw her at Driscoll's table in her clean white gown. He saw her led by the cop at the station. He saw her refusing her last rights. He saw her in the courtroom and then screaming at him to run at the gallows. He saw her rocking on her seat on the train, looking wistfully out the window. He saw her bailing water as a boy on a boat. He saw her grinning in the crystal clear sea as she swam like a fish. And just as his heart filled with warmth, again he saw her dash across the jungle, yielding a murder weapon, dripping with blood. He was shaken; prickles covered his skin. He watched her walk away, unsure if he loved her or hated her.

30

Boat

"So, we have to steal a boat," Quinn said plainly as she stared up the beach line towards the small village that had welcomed Nevel just nights before.

Nevel didn't understand how she could move so quickly from bearing her soul to brainstorming, but he was relieved at the change in topics. He wanted to leave her here, he wanted her to go with him; he didn't know what he wanted. He was tormented inside. For now, she would go with him. He would convince himself of the old adage "you keep your friends close and your enemies closer." Whichever she was he'd be a fool to let her loose while he still had work to do. He would refocus; his efforts wouldn't be for her or for himself. Every move would be as an agent of the UBM.

"We can't. It wouldn't be right," Nevel said. Nevel scratched the back of his neck while he thought. They had been so kind nursing Quinn back to health and taking Nevel in when he ran away. He couldn't steal from them.

Quinn rubbed her tired eyes and tried again. "OK, wrong choice of words. We borrow a boat. It's not stealing if you return it."

"And how do you return it?" Nevel rolled his eyes and plopped down in the sand.

"I don't know. Maybe we don't return it. Maybe we just leave it for them to pick up. We'll figure it out. We always do." Quinn sat next to him. Too close. She sat too close, Nevel thought to himself. He wasn't falling for her beguiling female tactics anymore. He was focused.

Nevel didn't like the idea of taking a boat from the people who had taken him in during his great breakdown just an evening before, but he knew Quinn was right. They had nothing to trade, a language barrier between them made any knowledge exchange impossible. Their island languages were not in any translation dictionary in the vault in his mind. These islanders were natural survivalists; Nevel and Quinn couldn't teach them anything they didn't already know. They began to plan as they sat in the sand, drawing routes with their fingers through the coarse grains. Quinn's leg was healing with the antibiotics, but they decided to keep the wrap on it just in case for another day or so.

"We'll go tonight. Night will be our cover. We'll

just wait until it's deep in the night and we're sure they're settled for good," Nevel said from his spot in the sand, which he refused to give up, despite the fact that she still sat too close. He wasn't moving for her. "When the torches are out and the bonfire turns to embers, we'll go." With that Nevel laid back and put his hands behind his head on the sand to wait out the night.

"Right," Quinn said quietly, mimicking his move by lying back in the sand. She didn't say a word, though, which was good, Nevel thought. In his opinion, she had said too much already today.

Nevel realized he must have nodded off because he was surprised to feel Quinn poking him in the ribs in the pitch black of night.

"Wake up!"

Quickly, Nevel sat up and looked down the beach at where the village was. He saw only black silhouettes of palm trees swaying and a faint outline of thatched huts in the moonlight. He couldn't even see the glowing remnants of a bonfire. Immediately, Nevel knew he had slept longer than intended and that time would be of the essence if they were to meet their goals for the evening.

Jumping to his feet and shaking off the sand, Nevel looked at Quinn and said, "Let's go," and then took off toward the village in a slow jog. Before, he would have asked her if she was ready, one of them would have made a quirky comment to set off their adventure. Now, the air was thick between them.

The jog up the beach was short and easy for Nevel. Quinn kept astride, not saying a word. When they arrived at the edge of the village, the whistling island winds and the hum of the jungle bugs were the only sounds they could hear. Nevel and Quinn tiptoed to the overturned canoes that lay on the sand by a rocky patch at the edge of the tribal village. Nevel was grateful that the boats were kept far from the huts; he felt the plan could go off without a hitch. With Quinn at the bow and Nevel at the stern, they lifted the tree trunk boat in unison along their right side and flipped it over. It was not as heavy as Nevel had imagined it would be, so he was relieved the lift wasn't a struggle for the two. For a fleeting moment, he realized it may have been difficult to complete this task without her, but then again, he had grown strong. Nevel had worried about the sound it would make when they flipped it, but the sound merged with all of the other natural sounds of the island: the wind, moving water, and whispering palms. Under the boat, two long paddles lay in the sand. Nevel grabbed them with one fist and set them quietly within the boat. Again they lifted the boat in unison, one at each end, as they snuck towards the sea.

They moved silently to the water. Soon dry sand became cooler and wet beneath their footprints, and then slow waves splashed their ankles and shins. When the water reached Quinn's knees, she looked back at Nevel over her shoulder and then began to climb aboard as they had planned. Nevel steadied the rocking boat by leaning his midsection across both gunnels. The moonlight kept her in sight as he watched her lift her body in, but a rogue wave surprised them both and she was sent splashing back into the water.

Nevel looked at the black sea that swallowed her and held his breath. He didn't hate her. He needed her. The feeling in his chest for the seconds she disappeared screamed to him that he loved her. There she was, he saw her hand on the side of the boat. He looked over his shoulder to the huts for movement. The village remained still. He looked at the water. She was surfacing and trying to board the small boat again, this time with success. It was Nevel's turn. If he fell in, his swimming might not be strong enough to send him back to try again as Quinn had. He would have to make it in the boat on the first try without anyone steadying the boat for him.

Nevel grabbed the gunnels and lifted himself into the boat in one quick move. His strong arms surprised him. Inside, he stumbled to his knees and grabbed a paddle. The boat was rough on his knees, but he ignored any pain. He gripped the paddle with clenched fists and dug it into the water with a powerful force, the same almost inhuman force that thrust him into the boat. Immediately, they were paddling against the waves toward escape. The sides of the boat were low and the waves were not merciful. Though the sea was calm, the small waves were enough to send the boat rocking and skidding across the surface. Quinn and Nevel paddled, though the dark and Nevel's nerves sent them out of sync and fighting with each other as well as the current. His kneecaps were burning from the way they were scraping the bottom of the boat and the salt from the seawater stung his wounds.

They were going over the waves and out to sea,

but the canoe was turning now. One moment he was facing shore, another moment he was facing the sea. Nevel worried they had made a mistake. This wouldn't work. His hands were shaking. He was no match for this water. Any moment they could tip and they were getting pulled far enough out now that he wouldn't be able to touch ground if he went overboard. His fingernails were cutting into his own palms where they gripped the paddle.

"One, two, one, two, one, two," Quinn began to call from her seat in the bow. She was sitting on her bottom. Nevel followed her lead and was relieved to be off his knees. Now he had a more stable and pain-free position in the vessel. He dipped and pushed back against the water on her command as she continued to call, "One, two, one, two." Who was he kidding? He couldn't have done this without her. He wondered if he could do anything without her.

His heart beat in this rhythm. Was she calling him out on his rapid heartbeat, his fear? No, she was paddling to the rhythm. Quickly, he snapped out of his fear coma and joined her.

"One, two, one, two, one, two,"

Soon they took the control of the vessel back from the sea and were moving with momentum in a straight line towards the dark mountain as they paddled in unison. Nevel could breathe again. The rocking was steadied now as they pushed forward through the dark. They charged towards the black mountain silhouette across the sea.

Nevel didn't talk much to Quinn. His mind was filled with images of sharks. He had read too much about the Great Whites off the Australian coast and he knew well the waters were full of them. Every terrified thought sent Nevel paddling harder and the boat moved with such momentum forward that it almost appeared to have a small motor at the back. They weren't paddling for more than forty-five minutes when they were riding the surf waves into their destination beach.

31
Arrival

It was terrifying arriving on a black beach in the dead of night. This mountain island had been their view from their lagoon across the water for several nights and it was always dark, which meant no village people lighting torches or bonfires. This island should be uninhabited, Nevel thought.

Just moments after pulling the boat onto the sand, the mosquitoes started to attack them. They were relentless, bombarding them in swarms. Swatting at them did nothing. Nevel and Quinn moved from the sand and back into the water, diving under the waves to rid themselves of the persistent bugs that covered them from head to toe. The water was the only place they were safe from the biting pests.

"What are we going to do?" Quinn asked as she itched all over in the water where the mosquitoes had already left dozens of irritating red bumps all over her body. "They even got under my clothes!"

Nevel was equally uncomfortable, splashing water over his bare chest to rinse the bites and reaching into his shorts to itch.

"We can't stay in the water. We need to cover our skin in mud. It will be a barrier. If it is thick enough, they won't be able to penetrate it," Nevel said but dreaded leaving the water again to follow his own suggestion.

"OK," Quinn said reluctantly and they again waded to the dark beach. They immediately fell under attack as they reached the water's edge. They ran toward the jungle's edge to dig in the ground for mud, swatting and scratching.

"Ugh!" Quinn complained.

"Here—mud!" Nevel slapped a handful to Quinn who slapped it on her face and body as fast as she could. Nevel dug for more and she joined him on her hands and knees.

The ground was easy to penetrate. It was moist and the mud was clay-like from all the precipitation in the rainforest. Their hands scooping like shovels, they painted themselves as fast as they could as the invisible predators continued their wrath. They ignored the crawling beetles and wiggling worms that sometimes invaded their handfuls of mud. The mosquitoes were so irritating that nothing else mattered except covering themselves to ease their discomfort.

"It's starting to work," Quinn said as she continued lathering on layers and layers of mud to her arms, face, legs, and stomach.

"Yeah, I'm not feeling them as much anymore," Nevel agreed, almost finished covering his chest and legs and face with the thick clay barrier. "How's your leg?" Nevel asked, checking on Quinn.

"It's fine, better, really," she said as she tightened Nevel's shirt around it again.

After a few moments of mud painting, they stopped and looked at each other.

"Better?" Nevel asked.

"Yeah, better," Quinn replied, "You're a genius. Who knew mud would do the trick?"

"I did." Nevel laughed and Quinn rolled her eyes at his joke. "It's night, I know, but I'm not that tired. You want to try to move as far as we can tonight?" Nevel asked Quinn. Truly, he would feel like a sitting duck if they decided to set up camp on the shore. Here they would sit with a stolen boat, directly across from the tribe from which they stole it. Surely, the tribe could hop on their other boats and come after them. Nevel hoped not, but he was a realist.

"Let's hide the boat first. I know we are leaving it for them to find and pick up, but if it's too obvious we may run into problems. We need to buy ourselves some time," Quinn said and Nevel agreed. They pulled their vessel up to the edge of the forest and began to cover it with vines and palms and any brush they could until it looked like just a part of the groundcover.

"Good, can't see it at all." Nevel looked at Quinn who was swatting at the mosquitoes unconsciously even though they weren't penetrating her skin any-more.

"OK, let's make tracks while we're up," Quinn agreed and they started moving into the jungle.

It was thick with forest. Trees were so tall, like none Nevel had ever seen. The canopies seemed to touch the sky. Luckily tonight the moon was bright and sent splinters of light through the forest so they could see. Their clay cover made them look tribal, the whites of their eyes beamed against their camouflage like a panther's eyes glowing in the black of night.

"What if we see nothing from up there? What if..." Quinn asked.

"These are the only instructions we were given. The captain said we would be picked up in a week from the other side of this mountain. Maybe it was their plan all along. I don't know, Quinn. I'm just as lost as you. For all we know, the UBM has had a ship there waiting for us for days. All I know is the UBM is sending us a ship and we've got to find it. I don't know. Got any better ideas?" Nevel wished he had softened his tone a bit, but his frustration was welling. Why hadn't the UBM sent them any sort of more specific message with the captain? Had they been tricked? Were they supposed to be on The Lillian Ruth right now? Was Nevel still supposed to have the Register? He checked his shorts for the Pass of the Crow.

They walked in quiet for a long time. Nevel was lost in thought. The dark of the rainforest wasn't conducive to conversation anyway as the constant hum of the insects and frogs rang in their ears. Their footing was difficult, as the density of the forest seemed to leave no natural trails. Often they had to swim their arms through webs of vines to clear enough space for their bodies to pass through. Lucky for them, they knew they were heading up due to the slope. Otherwise, they would have been helplessly lost.

Nevel was surprised when he began to shiver. Being both wet and covered in thick mud, Nevel felt like he was in a refrigerator in the dark. He knew tomorrow the sun would dry his mud coating and he would complain of heat inside a shell casing, but now the mud was still moist and was making him cold. He was happy for the physical activity that kept him warm, but he did start to worry about Quinn again.

"Are you OK?" he asked. "It's getting pretty cold."

"I'm good," she lied through chattering teeth.

"We will just have to keep moving to stay warm. Won't be long until the sun comes up." Nevel hoped they had only an hour or two left of darkness.

Moving through the dark of the outback had scared Nevel, but it was at least still his turf. Nevel knew about a lot of the dangers that lurked in the rainforests here from the books in his mind, but he also was humble enough to know he didn't have a home field advantage. Nevel knew there were plenty of perils surrounding them now—perhaps even stalking them—that he couldn't even begin to identify. He pulled the knife from its hiding place in his shoe and gripped it tight in his fist as he moved closer to Quinn so as not to leave any space between them as they hiked up the jungle mountain.

The pitch dark here was unlike that of their island lagoon from previous nights. Their beach had the expected sounds: the lapping of waves, the hum of insects, the rustling of the wind through the palms. Here, in the thick of this mountain jungle, the sounds and even the darkness seemed heavier. Thuds, cracks, booms echoed above the light songs of bugs and winged creatures. Strange howls and low growls leapt from every corner. The hairs on the back of Nevel's neck stood on end. And then, even more terrifying than the sounds that had filled his ears, a sudden silence fell across the jungle. Nevel held his hand up to stop Quinn in her tracks. She bumped into him; the darkness had hidden his cue to stop.

Suddenly the ground beneath Nevel's feet began to shake and tremble. His calves vibrated and sent tremors up his thighs and spine. Instinctively, he first looked down at his feet and the undulating soil. Even in the dark, he could see the movement. Then he looked at Quinn. She too, was looking down, shaking like she was standing on a crumbling sand dune.

"What's happening?" Quinn looked up at Nevel. All he could see were the whites of her eyes, but they were wide in fear, "Is it a volcano? Is it about to erupt?" She didn't grab his hand. He didn't reach for her. He thought about it, but he didn't. They stood apart on shaky ground. "No, the volcano was on the other island," Nevel replied, still trying to figure out what was happening, "It's got to be an earthquake. An aftershock from the MegaCrash." It wasn't uncommon for them to feel tremors in Morgan Creek even a decade after the MegaCrash, so it shouldn't be any different here. This seemed stronger, though.

Though they couldn't see them, they could hear the cracks and booms of trees falling. Branches fell all around them, some swatting them in the face with leaves and brush as they fell. Nevel had to bend his knees and squat to keep from falling over. Quinn took a step closer to him; her knees too were bent. She almost didn't make it to him without falling. Nevel wondered what it would be worth, what any of what he had been through would be worth if he hadn't been through it with her. He wanted to jump towards her and wrap his arms around her and protect her, but just as he considered it, the ground settled and became as still as the humid air that still hung thick between them.

Perhaps only a minute had passed during the time the ground started shaking. The vibrations echoed through Nevel's body even as he now stood still.

"That's it. You ok?" Nevel checked on Quinn.

"Fine, you're right. Just tremors." Quinn was stepping in circles as if to check the ground to be sure it was really still now.

Finally, the black sky lightened to a gray and then pinks and oranges streaked through the jungle like streamers and started a new day. Immediately, Nevel began to feel the comfort of warmth and as the heat set in, he felt tired for the first time.

"We have to rest," Nevel said and Quinn yawned, nodding in agreement.

"Up off the ground is safer," Nevel pointed to a tree and the low branches made it easy to climb. The twisting of the vines acted almost as a hammock and

Nevel laid back and instinctively, without thinking, opened his arm to invite Quinn to lie in the crutch of his chest. In moments they were asleep.

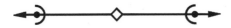

Nevel awoke to a tickling feeling. He dreamed Tank was licking his leg and a wide grin flashed across his sleeping face. Then it was more of a squeeze and Nevel lurched awake and lifted his chin off his chest to look down at his leg. A boa was snaking a loop around his calf, its tongue dashing up and down to explore his scent. Quinn was on his chest asleep. Nevel tapped her on the head.

"Oh, sorry, I hope I didn't drool..." Nevel cut Quinn off as he motioned for her to move and then pointed at his leg.

"Oh no," Quinn yanked her legs into her chest, avoiding contact with the snake herself.

"Quinn, you're going to have to kill it," Nevel said in as calm a voice as he could muster as he handed her the knife that was still in his grip.

"Right, no worries," Quinn said, but there was worry in her voice.

This snake was easily six feet long and five inches thick, probably small for this rainforest, Nevel thought. It was coiling itself around his shin and moving toward his knee. The squeeze was beginning to slowly tighten.

Quinn perched herself on the branch and attempted to find her balance as she gripped the knife and waddled toward the snake. The snake stilled at her movement and looked at her while tightening its squeeze. Nevel held his breath. He couldn't look. She could stab at the snake and miss and he could have a knife in one of his main arteries, but the snake was squeezing him harder now and he could feel his pulse beat in his calf so he knew he had to let it be done. Quinn moved slowly. She was a hunter; Nevel could find comfort in that. Suddenly Nevel felt Quinn lunge and heard her scream. He kept his eyes closed and clenched his teeth. The squeeze let loose. He opened his eyes. Quinn tossed the snake's head to the ground and lifted the long, limp body.

"Breakfast!" she proudly announced.

The relief Nevel felt sent the breath he had been holding rushing out of his mouth and his clenched muscles limp.

"I am so glad you have Driscoll blood!"

"Let's see what we can do about cooking this bad boy!"

Everything in the rainforest was so damp.

"Nothing will be dry enough to burn," Nevel admitted finally after they had both spent time in a fruitless search.

"Yeah, the sticks are all soaking wet," Quinn agreed.

"Shame to toss it, but if we can't cook it…"

"Yeah and carrying it is only going to slow us down."

Quinn dropped the snake and found the silver lining, "Well, at least it didn't kill ya."

Nevel laughed and they moved on. They walked,

the sun drying their mud coats into shells as Nevel had expected. Soon after they recommenced their trek, Quinn held up her hand, stopping Nevel in his tracks.

"Shhh," Quinn hushed Nevel, pushing him back behind a tree with her outstretched arm.

Nevel fell back as requested, but he was confused. He looked around and didn't see anything. As they stood in silence, he didn't hear anything either other than the sounds of the jungle. The sunlight made it very easy to see and he saw nothing around them.

"What is it?" Nevel asked.

"I swear I heard people talking, in the distance." Quinn was looking around, paranoid and pale.

"You're just dehydrated. Your mind is playing tricks on you. There's no one on this island. Maybe it was a bird."

"I know what I heard. There are people here." Quinn was adamant.

"We haven't seen any evidence of people on this island! No huts, no bonfires, no boats," Nevel reaffirmed.

"Shhh. There…" Quinn pointed up. "They're in the trees."

32

Trees

Quinn pointed up. Nevel couldn't believe what he saw. At least forty meters up, the tree branches had more of a specific pattern than usual. They were criss-crossing and weaving and even appeared to be topped by thatched roofs.

"Treehouses?" Quinn said as Nevel suddenly caught a glimpse of dark flesh-colored beings moving across the branches so far above.

He swallowed hard, terror-stricken.

"Amazing!" Quinn said pointing up at them, but Nevel was not excited at their find. He quickly pointed his finger to Quinn's mouth to quiet her and slowly guided her down to the ground to crouch behind a bush. He had read of the Karowai and Kombai tribes, known as the "tree people." They were known for one exceptional trait: cannibalism.

"Quinn, we have to get out of here." Nevel tugged at her shirt to get her attention. The material had grown thin from the water and sun. Even from this hiding place, she continued to gawk up, using her hand to shield her eyes to better see the fortresses high above them.

"Maybe they're friendly," she whispered, not sensing Nevel's urgency as she pushed the branches of the bush to one side to get a better view of the life in the trees high above, "Maybe they could help us."

"Quinn," Nevel turned her head with his hands to force her to look his way. "I have read about these tribes that live in treehouses in the jungles of Papua New Guinea. Believe me, they're not going to help us." Nevel didn't want to frighten Quinn by revealing their unique palate.

"Well, we'll just keep moving, maybe they won't notice us," she whispered, looking up again and beginning to stand.

Nevel yanked her back down by pulling her shirt.

"Quinn, they can't notice us," Nevel realized he would have to tell her. She needed to be afraid; it was now a matter of safety. "They are cannibals."

"What?" Her look of curiosity quickly changed to one of fear. Now she was listening to Nevel. Quinn's face went pale, "Oh, OK," she said and she shook her head in disbelief.

"We're going to change direction," Nevel whispered and she nodded in stunned agreement.

Nevel pulled her arm and they crept their way

backwards into the deep, lush forest as quietly and carefully as they possibly could, all the while keeping their eyes up and on the people running through the treehouse mazes high above.

"Do you think they saw us?" Quinn finally whispered as the view of the treehouses slowly disappeared and they straightened their crouching bodies to standing again.

"No, I don't think they did," Nevel said, still moving with an air of caution. They headed the other direction, still up the mountain, but now towards the east instead of west.

"How can you be sure?" Quinn asked, looking up.

"No treehouses above us right now," Nevel replied. "Now let's pick up the pace." Nevel was ready to pick up speed and get off this island as fast as possible. He focused on the climb and moved forward, keeping Quinn ahead so he could keep an eye on her.

After a while, Nevel's shins were tight from the arduous semi-sprint uphill. Quinn moved ahead of him so quickly now, he was having trouble keeping up. Her leg had obviously improved immensely and the fear of cannibalism understandably helped inspire her speed as well.

Nevel paused to stretch his calf and watched Quinn disappear into the rays of sunlight that blinded him from above. He didn't want to shout to her to wait with the treehouses still not far enough in the distance. They had agreed to hike in silence. Nevel figured Quinn would eventually look over her shoulder and realize he wasn't there and backtrack a bit until they reconnected. The sharp splinters of pain in his shin gave him no choice but to stop and stretch.

Pressing the ball of his right foot firmly against a fallen tree trunk, Nevel pushed his heel down and shifted his weight forward in a lunge over his right knee. He could feel the muscles lengthening like rubber bands and momentarily the pain subsided. After a good, long stretch, he switched feet and pressed his left heel down while lunging over his left leg. The stretch was releasing the tension and recharging Nevel to continue. Just as he was about to release the lunge and continue on, Nevel heard a rustling noise from the groundcover behind him.

Quickly, he turned. His chin dropped and his breath hung in the air. He was looking at a man like no man he had ever seen before.

33
Prey

Crouching low to the ground on all fours, like a panther about to pounce, a man of the jungle glared at Nevel with white eyes that pierced from the dark skin of his face. He was naked except for a shell covering that looked like a bird's beak over his pelvic area. His dark body was painted in white lines around his thick biceps and away from his cheekbones on his face like whiskers. Black lines circled his eyes and white dots adorned his chest. He chattered something through his sharp teeth.

"HITCHATCHI CHA DIOABO." It came out through clenched teeth, in a sort of hiss.

Nevel's skin crawled. He stood very still. A fly buzzed by his eye, but Nevel didn't dare wave it away.

The man remained in his warrior's position, but shifted his head left and then right atop his shoulders, as he looked Nevel over. A bead of sweat ran down the man's back beneath his shell casing.

Nevel wondered if this man was alone. He hoped and prayed he was alone. Though Nevel couldn't understand the language the man spoke, he did seem to be speaking to or at least at Nevel and not to another as he didn't raise his voice and call out.

Again the man hissed from his clenched teeth, "HITCHATCHI CHA DIOABO." This time the man crawled forward, right arm and leg slowly forward, wrist hooked under, followed by the left side. He moved like an animal, Nevel thought. He didn't even seem human. His movement revealed a harpoon of sorts in his right hand. It was a piece of bamboo, about four feet in length, which had been camouflaged by the jungle floor in their stare-off. At its tip was a sharp shell in the shape of an arrow. Nevel swallowed and blinked, but didn't dare do anything more. Quinn had his knife after her snake kill. He was weaponless. The man crept up to Nevel like a predator sniffing an unknown prey; his eyes and nose were taking in this Aussie stranger.

He began examining Nevel's shoes and bare ankles, which were no longer covered by the mud that blanketed most of the rest of Nevel as it had worn well off in the hiking. The man looked at Nevel's white ankle skin and poked it with his index finger. Nevel scanned the jungle while he stood being inspected. No one was in sight. Not additional tribal men, not Quinn either. He worried if she too had been found or if she was just hiking on completely oblivious to the threat. This man seemed to be made of instincts and Nevel feared he couldn't outsmart him in his home territory.

The man picked at the mud covering Nevel's legs and watched it crumble and come off at each poke of his finger. This seemed to anger and confuse the man as he quickly moved from his crouch to a full standing position that brought him face to face with Nevel.

"Kichoma!" he said inches from Nevel's face, the whites of his eyes glaring at Nevel. His teeth were sparse and riddled with black spots, his gums darker than his skin. Then he scratched at Nevel's face, causing the mud barrier to break down and crumble off, revealing his white skin.

Immediately the mosquitoes swarmed and Nevel tried to be still, but he couldn't help but blink and shake his head to avoid the pests. The tribesman watched and narrowed his eyes before reaching to the ground and grabbing at something. Nevel clinched his fists and gritted his teeth, preparing to accept a blow from his spear. Instead, the man wiped Nevel's face with an oily leaf that immediately sent the mosquitoes fleeing. Its odor opened Nevel's nostrils and singed the hairs in his nose, but the mosquitoes were gone. Nevel looked to see the man holding a plant he had just plucked from the ground, the obvious source of the oil repellant.

Perhaps the man was friendly, Nevel hoped for a moment. Perhaps Nevel wasn't right. The books in his mind referred to the tree people as cannibals, but they were in fact history books. Time had passed. Perhaps these people had changed their ways. Perhaps there was nothing to fear at all. Nevel's thoughts were immediately jarred to reality as the man pushed him to the jungle floor and tied his hands behind his back with a vine he ripped from the ground.

34

Vines

Nevel walked with a spear pressed into his back. He couldn't help but almost laugh at the absurdity of it all: just months before he had been in a similar situation with Quinn pressing him forward through the outback. His captor whistled and the long, smooth tune flooded the jungle and floated up to the treetops. Nevel was scared. He knew this was a summons to the others, the cannibals in the trees.

He looked up and saw no treehouses yet. This was a slight comfort. He knew they had further to travel and hoped they were indeed trekking back to the tree village he had spotted earlier, that there weren't more treehouse villages here in this part of the jungle. Nevel had been paying close attention to that. His memory served him well and he expected they would have at least three more miles to go before returning to the treehouses from before if that was indeed the destination.

The man did not crawl now, but walked upright. Nevel tried to look back over his shoulder on occasion to get a glimpse. Each time he was given only a second's look, but it was enough to picture his captor in his mind; He was shorter than Nevel, lean, but with muscular arms and thighs. A horn from some sort of animal covered his manhood and bones hung around his neck; one pierced right through his nose. His ankles jingled when he walked with the shells tied to them and Nevel wondered why he hadn't heard him coming earlier. Suddenly the man began to chant, a low muttered song that kept pace with their walking. Nevel could not make any sense of it other than that it was perhaps a working song—maybe even a hunting song. It was eerie, otherworldly.

Nevel scanned the library in his mind to find out more about these cannibalistic tree-dwellers, but every sentence he read did more frightening than enlightening and he gave up on the quest for information about their habits and genealogy as an avenue for escape from this danger.

Nevel knew if he was going to escape it would have to be now, before being presented to the tribe, which would outnumber and out-power him easily. He immediately put off any thought of escape through communication. He considered running, but something told him the dagger that was currently at his back would be through him before he could take his first step. Still, without a weapon, running was the only possibility. Nevel had become a fast runner over the last few months in a quest to remain alive, but this man was animalistic and might be able to outrun a jaguar for all Nevel knew.

As he weighed his options, Nevel heard a sound in the distance that filled him with hope.

"CAWCAW!"

The captor stopped in his tracks and looked in the direction of the sound. Immediately Nevel's thoughts of hope turned back to fear. She was in danger too now. Nevel's bare ankles crawled with ants. He kicked at the air to rid himself of them and the native captor smacked him to the ground with the shaft end of the bamboo. Suddenly, Nevel was lying in a mound of ants that covered his mud casing as if he were already a corpse. He was glad again of his mud cover, but soon the ants began finding the cracks; infiltration ensued. Nevel could not stop wriggling in an attempt to rid himself of the ant infestation. The captor placed his foot on Nevel's chest to still him, but Nevel couldn't control his reaction to the ants. He ripped off chunks of his shell casing, wiping his body feverishly with his hands to toss the ants off of him. His captor watched in confusion, pointing the spear at him with a face of intimidation. Bending and breaking the mud casing, an unstoppable Nevel was almost free. He dropped and rolled, finally ridding himself of the pests in a lush patch of green fern. His captor kept the spear pointed at Nevel, with wide eyes. As Nevel finally stopped, his captor scanned the trees for the sound.

"CAWCAW!" There it was again. Closer now. Did she see him? Did she know he was there? With a captor? Should he return her call or would that just enrage his captor or endanger her more?

The native looked at Nevel and cocked his head to the side in confusion. A flash of red burst through the trees behind him. *She's alone*, he thought in relief. Now he knew she was trying to save him.

Nevel's captor pointed up a tree and poked Nevel in the tender flesh below his ribcage with the spear. He wanted Nevel to climb. This was not good, Nevel thought. The trees were his captor's territory. Nevel moved slowly to the tree, buying time, scanning for Quinn. There was the spear again in his flesh, this time pushing to leave a mark. Nevel grabbed a low limb and pulled himself up with both biceps far enough to leverage his left leg to place it on another branch to push himself up. In the time it took Nevel to make his one arduous move, his captor had leapt up beside him with ease like a tree monkey. He pointed above, urging Nevel to continue on. The native seemed irritated at Nevel's slothfulness. Nevel could climb better, he had scaled a rock the size of a sky-scraper in the outback, but he used his non-native dis-abilities as a chance to buy time. He scanned the for-est for Quinn or others as he and his captor slowly as-cended the tree.

The rainforest was thick with twisting branches of lush green groundcover hiding the muddy floor and shaded by the green canopy top that sent shards of sunlight across it like scattered puzzle pieces. The fur-ther they climbed, the harder it was to make out the images below. Sounds filled his ears: bugs buzzing, branches swaying and cracking under the weight of flying birds and monkeys, whistles and echoes of animals unknown.

Nevel looked to his captor: he was barefoot and the soles of his feet wrapped around the branches he traversed like an animal, gripping and swinging from limb to limb with ease. The trees were his home, clearly; this was evidenced not only by his skill but also by his passion for moving through them.

He handed Nevel a coarse vine and pointed across.

"Swing?" Nevel asked in disbelief out loud, knowing they couldn't communicate verbally.

Again, his captor held out the vine, this time pressing it into Nevel's palm and pushing his fingers to close around it. Nevel looked down. They were at least thirty feet up now. A fall would most definitely cause serious injury. Nevel knew he was no match for this tree-man in terms of escaping on his turf, but escape was imminent.

There were no calls from Quinn. He did not see other tree-men. She must be near, he thought, stalking them under the cover of the jungle. Nevel wondered if he pushed his captor would he fall or catch himself with his agile skills? Time was not on Nevel's side. He had to do something now if he wanted to escape.

Nevel took the vine and looked with exaggerated nervousness at the tree-man urging him to swing. He would use this, Nevel thought. He adjusted his grip on the vine several times and looked down and then back into the face of the tree-man. He slid his fists apart on the stretch of vine, leaving a good length. He took a long breath in. His hands were shaking. He wasn't nervous about a jump. He was nervous about what he was about to do to his captor.

Nevel pushed himself from squatting to standing, still with two fists clenching the vine. His captor pointed. Nevel gave him a look dripping with nerves. The tree-man sidled up closer to Nevel, perhaps to give him a nudge to force him to swing. This was the action Nevel had anticipated. In one fell swoop, Nevel wrapped the vine in a noose around his captor's neck and pulled. The tree-man was caught in surprise. His eyes bulged as his breath was stolen. Nevel pulled and wrapped, trying not to look him in the eye. His fists were clenched so tight, what was left of the mud dust that still covered parts of his skin began to crumble and fall. The tree-man reached for Nevel's neck in protest, but he was surprised and flailing and unable to reach Nevel. Never had Nevel been in a position to take someone's life. He didn't want to. He was a visitor here. This was wrong. But it was Nevel or his captor, a cannibal in the wilds of Papua New Guinea. Nevel fought for his life as he squeezed until the man became deadweight and no longer struggled; Nevel was supporting a limp body. He let go, hands shaking as he looked at the man whose eyes were still wide in surprise, but whose breath was gone—taken by Nevel. He whispered, "Forgive me." A tear slid down his face. He propped the body in a sitting position in the crook of the tree and climbed down as fast as he could with a quiet "CAWCAW."

He was shaking. At the base of the tree, he looked

up. He could see the body of the tree-man perched in the tree. The body was still. Nevel wished for a moment that he would see it jerk awake, forcing Nevel to run for his life, but also allowing him comfort in that fact that he hadn't actually taken the life of a man with his hands. Nevel stared. The body lay still. Nevel shook his head and rubbed his eyes. *Get it together,* he thought to himself, *find Quinn. Get out of here.*

Nevel started in a slow jog away from the tree where his captor lay dead. He didn't have any idea where he was running. The library in his mind was open. He was scanning books for the right words to help him through his remorse. He found a quote from Euripides. "Death is a debt we all must pay." Nevel knew he had faced a situation in which only one could be victor. Though his heart ached at his act, the words helped him through it. The tree-man had paid a debt Nevel would one day also pay. Nevel had to remind himself that it wasn't just his own life he was protecting, but the life of the UBM. He would have to move on now if he was to make it to the pick-up. He couldn't help but think that he and Quinn now shared another bond, one that made him cringe; murder.

Just as his mind began to clear and his jogging became more swift and purposeful, he saw Quinn running toward him.

"I saw it all. I was trying to figure out how to help. Are you OK?" Quinn whispered at their reunion.

"I'm fine," Nevel said, but he was lying. The face of his victim was burned in his brain.

"We've got to get out of here," Quinn reminded

him, pulling on his arm towards the direction from which she had come.

She was right, Nevel knew that. They started off in a slow jog, Quinn pulling Nevel by the arm as he snapped out of his dazed state. The jog turned into a sprint up the mountain. They were running out of time if they were to make it to the other side for pick-up.

The particular mountain path they now were forced to take was muddy with so many canopies shading the groundcover that was surely pelted with rain on a regular basis. Sprinting through this part of the jungle was unbearable. After losing their shoes time and time again in thick, sticky mud, they tied them over their shoulders and moved on with bare feet. When the ground finally became easier to traverse, as it grew dryer closer to the top of the mountain, the jungle itself thickened to a point where it was almost impenetrable. Thick foliage grew from the floor of the jungle to its patched ceiling.

Their sprint slowed to a walk. Both Quinn and Nevel were out of breath. Nevel's body ached and the mosquitoes were at it again. Quinn's limp was worsening. The constant song of bugs, birds, and frogs never ceased.

"We've got to be close to the top," Nevel tried to encourage Quinn who was almost at a standstill.

Then, suddenly, a gray haze blanketed the forest. The trees began to sway. The leaves began to turn up their palms and reached to the sky begging for a drink. The wind blew in and thunder rolled and echoed. First tiny pellets, then sheets of water poured from the sky and into the forest. Instinctively, they both tilted their chins to the sky and opened their dry mouths to drink the rain. Quinn's mud suit was now washed from her body.

"Ahhh, my skin can breathe again," she called. Nevel just nodded in agreement as he relished the shower.

Though the island was hot, the rain was cold and so when the rain met the hot ground, a layer of steam arose and hung between the sheets of rain. A fog hung above, perhaps the steam rising formed clouds immediately above them. Nevel was surprised by the change in appearance of the jungle in a matter of moments with the onset of the rain. A quiet hush fell with the rain, pushing all the jungle creatures into holes and crevices. Nevel reveled in the cooling of his many bug bites and was happy to see the flying pests disappear in the rain. The groundcover of the jungle floor changed—the dead leaves were washed aside and the green of the moss and ferns shone with a new luster as the dirt and grime of the jungle floors was washed from it.

"Let's walk." Nevel pushed Quinn on through the dense, wet jungle.

The mud turned from sticky to slippery and Nevel knew they would need to pause their hike yet again. They were fighting mudslides and impermeable jungle curtains in a losing battle trying to make it uphill during a storm.

"Let's climb up this palm and wait it out," Nevel called through the sheets of rain that made it difficult to see or hear Quinn who was only a few feet ahead of him.

"OK," he thought he heard her reply.

He folded his hands and offered them for her to place her foot in to get a boost up into the tree. As soon as she was up, Nevel wrapped his arms around the thick branch on which she sat and flipped himself up like a gymnast.

In the tree, they managed to scoot to a spot on the thick branch that seemed to be more shielded from the rain due to a thick twisting of branches and palms right above it. Nevel grabbed a coconut.

"Got the knife?" he asked and Quinn gladly handed it to him. He split the coconut, offering Quinn half. They drank the little bit of coconut milk it offered before passing the knife back and forth to whittle bits of its flesh to eat. Quinn rested her head on Nevel's shoulder and they waited out the rain. It was too loud to talk and he was glad of it. He wouldn't know what to say. He still didn't know what to say to his Quinn.

The rain left as fast as it had come and the sun swooped in. Nevel and Quinn dropped from the tree and tried to move on despite the makings of many mudslides on their path. With the return of the sun came the return of the relentless mosquitoes. Quickly, Nevel and Quinn dropped to their knees and began scooping mud, which was easy to find after the showers, and re-covered their bodies to protect from the biting pests. Once they were covered, they continued to move up the slippery, muddy mountain.

"Try to walk on the ferns," Nevel suggested as they tried anything to get more traction in their attempts to reach the summit of this lush green mountain.

Always, Nevel continued to look over his shoulder and up into the trees to make sure they were not being stalked. Though he did not see anyone, often he felt he was being watched.

35

Summit

"How many days have passed since The Lilian Ruth left?" Nevel asked Quinn as they moved steadily up the mountain. They knew they were moments from the top now as the dense thick growth began to clear and expose a brilliant view of the sky.

"Five, I think, maybe six," Quinn replied. The chatter of birds and hum of insects forced them to speak up in order to hear each other.

"I see the top!" Nevel shouted as he ran forward, pointing to a mossy rock in a clearing. He was exhausted yet relieved. Panting and out of breath, the sweat he tasted was sweet victory. Reaching the mountain summit meant they would catch a glimpse of their pick-up. It meant the start of the next leg of their journey. Nevel wondered where it would take them. He was glad he had forgiven Quinn; he didn't want to do this alone.

"Come on!" he called to Quinn as he ran on, reaching his hand behind him for her to grab. She grabbed it and squeezed twice.

Together, they reached the mossy rock. As Nevel had expected, they could see over the mountain to the other side. The canopy of green trees that went down the other side of the mountain looked exactly like the side they had just climbed up, thick and lush but shorter in length and steeper. The water of the sea below was darker than that of their crystal clear lagoon, which probably meant it was deep, probably also the reason this would be their pick-up location—the perfect place for a ship to anchor. There was no ship there yet, which was a relief. It meant they still had time to descend. They hadn't yet missed their pick-up. The sandy white beach on the other side of the mountain was larger and void of tribal villages as far as Nevel could see. There were no footprints on the sand, no evidence that a boat had come looking for them and had left without them.

He spun around three-hundred-and-sixty degrees and looked at where they had been and where they may be going. Green lush mountains, puffing volcanoes, seas in every shade of blue, thatched huts, palms swaying, distant lands on the horizon—Nevel marveled at the beauty.

"Well, we made it to the top, now we have to head down, right?" Quinn said.

Nevel nodded his head, but he was still scanning

the horizon in search of what might be the ship that would carry them to their next destination. There weren't a lot of large sailing ships like The Lilian Ruth. He expected whatever it was, it would be a smaller sailboat.

The horizon was void of boats in every direction Nevel looked, but then Nevel saw something that confused him. Several objects, which looked like origami, black paper silhouettes against the sky. One, two, three, four, five, six, seven, eight, nine, ten.

"Look at all those ships!" Nevel pointed at the tiny shapes in the distance.

"Are you sure those are ships?"

"What else would they be?"

"What in the world?" Quinn was just as surprised as he was.

Nevel's mind spun, trying to make sense of it. Travel during this day and age was difficult and really only used for trade. Besides, when ships left for trade, they didn't travel in herds like that. Plus, sailboats stuck close to land for safety, they didn't travel so far out in the sea as they did long ago. Everything about what he was seeing didn't make sense.

"Is that our pick-up?" Quinn looked at Nevel. Nevel was staring at the chain of ships moving across the horizon.

"No way—too far out, too many." Nevel was trying to figure out what it meant.

Nevel opened maps in his mind. He knew the direction from which those ships were leaving and the direction to which they were heading and the maps confirmed it. It would make sense that a small place with a large urban population before the MegaCrash might run out of resources in this day and age. The ships were heading toward a place with plenty of space, a place to conquer and expand their power. His Australia.

"I think they might be Japanese war ships," a stunned Nevel said, shocked at the words falling from his lips.

"Do you mean they are going to attack? Aren't they headed right to Australia?"

"I'm afraid so, Quinn."

"Well, what do we do? We've got to do something! We have to warn someone..." Quinn was clearly worried.

"What can we do, Quinn? We are on an island," Nevel reminded her of the absurdity of her urgency. "We were in the city. We know they are ready for attack. Maybe they already know what's on the way. Anyway, there's nothing we can do other than to tell our pick-up when we see them and hope it's not news to them."

Quinn looked at Nevel with a nervous expression; rarely did she show vulnerability, fear. "Let's get going," Quinn said and started moving down the mountain. Nevel followed.

36

Renaissance

Nevel and Quinn moved faster down the other side of the mountain than their climb up the day before. They didn't talk much, Nevel had too much on his mind. He passed Quinn at one point without even realizing it. The wheels in his mind were turning, churning ideas and facts and hypothetical scenarios. War had always been a rumored threat; Nevel just didn't realize how real the threat was until he saw the ships with his own eyes. Maybe he was wrong, but his gut told him otherwise.

"Nevel, wait up," Quinn called. Nevel didn't mean to move so quickly down the mountain, but his feet were moving as fast as his brain. The same types of mudslides they had fought trying to climb up the mountain, were now helping them descend it as they rode sections down to quicken their pace. It was fun. Nevel was reminded of the slides at school when he was younger. He was happy that most of these mudslides landed in patches of fern to catch them. He stopped to wait for Quinn.

"Look!" She pointed at a small sailboat in the distance that was turning into the cove the mountain created, heading to the beach at the bottom. It was the type of sailboat that would have been someone's personal recreational boat before the MegaCrash. Now all boats were owned and operated by the government or military. Nevel squinted and could make out that there were about three sailors on the vessel with uniforms similar to the ones they wore on The Lillian Ruth. The new Australian flag whipped from the mast.

"They've got to be UBM if they are coming to pick us up, right?" Quinn asked. "But the flag?"

"Even UBM would fly that flag—to be safe, for cover," Nevel said. "It's got to be our pick-up. I have the Passes of the Crow, but we'll just have to feel them out, play along to whatever fits." Nevel grabbed Quinn's hand and she smiled in relief. He was taking her with him. He couldn't hate her. She loved him and he believed her. He loved her too, but he hadn't told her. Maybe she already knew. They continued their quick descent.

They ran, sliding still often, until the mudslides finally gave way to a green groundcover that preceded the sands of the beach. The thick lush ferns teemed with mosquitoes, which they kicked up with each step.

"I'm covered in the bloody pests," Quinn called out as she flailed her arms in swatting fashion. Nevel pulled the image from his mind of his tree-man captor and the plant he plucked with the oily repellent. He quickly scanned the ground and found a match. He pulled it and rubbed it all over his face and chest. The pungent smell flared in his nostrils, but the relief from the pests was well worth it.

"Here, rub this on you," Nevel said to Quinn as he extended his arm with a handful of the plant in his fist. Quinn took the bunch of green and began rubbing it all over her arms and face and legs.

"How did you figure this out? It's working!" Quinn sighed in relief as the thick swarm of mosquitoes dissipated.

"A little gift from the tree-people," Nevel replied as he continued coating his body with the repellant. "Good now? We need to keep moving. We are really close to the beach now. I can see the water through the palms up ahead."

Quinn nodded and Nevel moved on, knowing she was following close behind. Nevel jogged across ferns and fallen logs. He pushed through shrubs and dangling vines. The closer he grew to the water, the thinner the jungle became and the easier it was to move through it. Soon, the ferns and leaves underfoot gave way to patches of sand.

"The beach!" Quinn called as she finally saw the beach ahead and the two ran from the jungle and out onto the open white patch of sand.

"We made it!" Nevel said and Quinn wrapped her

arms around him and hugged him. They were both soggy with sweat and rain and mud from the mudslides. The strong smell of the oily plant that had saved them from mosquitoes was probably also masking their strong body odor, Nevel thought and was glad of it.

"Let's cool off and clean up," Quinn said, letting go of Nevel and moving with a skip in her step toward the sea. She had been like a fish back at their lagoon, always in the water swimming and reveling in the luxury of their private pool. Nevel smiled and followed to join her in the sea. He was now able to stay afloat since his swim lessons from Quinn in the lagoon at the start of this journey.

Wading in, Quinn immediately started splashing the water on her face and arms before reaching a depth where she could dive under and wash her whole body with the clean salt water. Nevel was still slower and more reluctant in the water, but he too waded in, washing his face and arms before dipping under when the depth allowed. It felt amazing to run his fingers through his hair under water and feel the mud and grime slip away. As they both washed, Nevel scanned the horizon again.

The sailboat was still a ways out, but now Nevel noticed something else.

"Look, another flag!" Nevel pointed at the ship, which was slowly growing closer.

"A crow!" Quinn smiled. A small white flag that looked just like the Pass of the Crow flew just below the New Australia flag. Now they knew for sure this was their pick-up.

"Let's go sit and wait," Nevel said, moving out of the water and to the beach with Quinn following, wringing out her clothes and hair.

They sat in the warm dry sand close together.

"It's been quite an adventure, Bookkeeper," Quinn said with a smirk.

"Yea, you could say that again," Nevel said, smiling back at her before returning his gaze to the sea.

"Quinn," Nevel said. They both sat with knees up, leaning back on their hands on the sand. She looked at him and waited for him to speak. He knew their hands were close enough to touch, but he didn't move. His mind returned to the page in *Great Expectations*; "*Love her, love her, love her! If she favours you, love her. If she wounds you, love her. If she tears your heart to pieces—and as it gets older and stronger, it will tear deeper—love her, love her, love her!*"

"What is it, Nevel?" Quinn waited.

He opened his mouth and nothing came out, not a word, not a feeling, not his heart on his lips.

"Never mind." He looked back out at the sea. The small vessel was approaching. The sailors on board waved at them, friendly, and Quinn and Nevel stood and waved back.

Nevel knew he needed to focus. The UBM needed him. He still had so many questions about what his mission would be. He thought about what he had assumed were war ships on the horizon. He thought about the Captain's words.

Placing the palms of his hands on the intricately carved twelve-foot mahogany door and then letting his fingers run along the face of Persephone before slowly pushing the door open, Nevel entered the library in his mind. This time he was not looking for a classic or a book of poetry, but a book more recently added to his collection. Nevel reached toward the rich, wood shelf where the Register now lay alone in a category all its own.

The book was thick with an embossed letter R on the cover and smelled of stretched animal hide. The pages were crisp, and somewhat wrinkled from the handmade scribing of quill and wet ink that dried and changed the consistency of the yellowed paper. The binding was stitched tight so that the book was difficult to open enough to get all the way to the inner crease. For this reason the margins had been made wide so as not to lose any of the words. The contents were just as Nevel had remembered; lists of titles with authors, publication dates, editions, and most importantly, locations where the book was checked in and out, next to dates.

Still, nothing in the Register seemed to stand out to Nevel to make it so incredibly important. Why would the location of the books be so crucial? Nevel scanned it and scanned it again. Still, he seemed to only be reading a library log of check in and check out dates with locations. No one book stood out with high importance.

He thought about the hidden message 'Let us exhume the culture of our past.' He thought about what the captain had said. The last question he had asked Nevel, "Don't you know what followed the dark ages?" And then it hit him. Like a ton of bricks, it finally hit him.

Nevel blinked. His mind spun. He saw the *Mona Lisa* hanging on a wall. He saw *Othello* and *Macbeth* being performed live on stage. He saw Michelangelo's *David* towering over him. He saw Milton's *Paradise Lost*. He saw Bacchus and Ariadne. Of course, the Renaissance! The Renaissance followed the Dark Ages of history. The Register suddenly had new meaning to Nevel.

Nevel reopened the Register in his mind and once again scanned the lists and lists of books he had scanned a hundred times. This time, however, his eyes were open for something else. Some of the titles now stood out, and checking their locations, it made sense. This was not only a list of where books were; it was also a list that told where masterpieces were hidden. Perhaps after the MegaCrash, books were confiscated and kept safe within the libraries, but what about the items that had once been housed by museums?

Nevel had read a book at some point—he struggled to remember what it was called—*The Digitization of Cultural Interaction*? It had a print date far prior to the MegaCrash. He searched his shelves madly for it. Left to right, his eyes scanned behind his closed lids. There! He found it, bound on a shelf high above his favorite classics, categorized simply under technology.

Nevel opened it and carefully read the introduction.

"No longer do the travelers and citizens of such a modern age wish to stand back and stare at relics and artifacts that are tucked safely behind glass. Citizens of today wish to touch the relics—smell them, move them in their hands! And why should they not?! Are we not to be able to interact with history in this day and age of modern technology?! No more velvet ropes in front of paintings! No more dinosaur bones hanging by wire above and out of reach! Introducing the newest experience in the history of museums: Digitized Historical and Cultural Interaction! Visitors at our modern digital museums will be able to climb aboard the replicated dinosaur and go for a ride! They will be able to feel the brush strokes in the *Mona Lisa* and even add their own brushstrokes to the ancient portrait! DHCI visitors will try on the Crown Jewels and will have a conversation with Joan of Arc!" Nevel couldn't believe he had forgotten about this book. He couldn't believe he hadn't thought of this before. Of course! So many items on the lists within the Register were books, but many were of actual relics themselves, items that had been stored away after the end of the traditional museums. The UBM would exhume the culture of the past by locating paintings and relics and ancient artifacts! He was a part of a worldwide treasure hunt!

"Nevel, you OK?" Quinn interrupted his train of thought.

"Yeah, just reviewing some things in my head. You know, preparing for the pick-up," Nevel returned to his mind.

Nevel read on. "Traditional museums are a dusty bore of the past! It is estimated that by the year 2020, all museums across the globe will become DHCI certified." And they must have, he thought. He had never been out of Morgan Creek, but he knew from the books in his mind about the great museums of the world: The Louvre, The Acropolis, The Metropolitan, The Smithsonian.

No wonder the Register was so important! He scanned the list again and came across not only titles of books, but now what he realized were titles of famous works: "The Mindenhall Treasure,"—the author was listed as "Romania" which Nevel knew was not an author, but a place of origin as this was a treasured relic of The Great Roman Empire. The location now for such relic was listed as Paris, France. Nevel stopped and thought. How many treasures were spread across this great world after the MegaCrash? The Register told Nevel a new story now. The UBM not only held books and knowledge, but they also held culture. Somehow, the UBM had managed to get to these relics before the governments of the world could. Somehow, they were keeping them hidden and passing them in secret in a movement towards humanism. Whoever had knowledge and culture would go beyond survival; they would thrive, like in the Renaissance. Whatever power could find these relics would certainly lead the world.

And Nevel had a list in his mind telling him the locations of every one.

Acknowledgements

Thank you to so many people in my life who have made this book possible. Thanks to my family for your constant support and love: To Punk for giving me the chance to chase my dreams; to Thomas and Eliza for inspiring me; to Mom, Dad, Britt, Andy, Charlie, Lindsey, Florian, Alexander, Karolina, MaryAnn, Arey, Christin, AW, Sam, Ben, Caroline, and all the aunts, uncles, and cousins whose love and support mean the world. Thanks to my friends and the people of Kinston for your support. Thanks to Frances Herring for her keen eye. Thanks to Julie Casey and Amazing Things Press for seeing the potential in a story I believe in so deeply.

Thanks to the readers who take this adventure with me and who are proof that the world still needs stories to take us places we may not otherwise be able to go.

About the Author:

Whitney L. Grady grew up in Warrenton, Virginia before leaving for college in North Carolina. She now lives in Kinston, North Carolina with her husband, two children, two dogs, and a cat. Whitney is a graduate of the University of North Carolina at Chapel Hill where she received a B.A. in English and East Carolina University where she received her Master's Degree in Education. *Pass of the Crow* is the second book in the *I Am Currency* series.

For updates on book signings and appearances, visit www.whitneylgrady.com.

A Message From the Author:

Thank you for taking the time to read my book. I would be honored if you would consider leaving a review for it on *Amazon*.

Check out these titles from
Amazing Things Press

Keeper of the Mountain by Nshan Erganian

Rare Blood Sect by Robert L. Justus

Evoloving by James Fly

Survival In the Kitchen by Sharon Boyle

Stop Beating the Dead Horse by Julie L. Casey

In Daddy's Hands by Julie L. Casey

How I Became a Teenage Survivalist by Julie L. Casey

Time Lost: Teenage Survivalist II by Julie L. Casey

Starlings by Jeff Foster

MariKay's Rainbow by Marilyn Weimer

Convolutions by Vashti Daise

Seeking the Green Flash by Lanny Daise

Nikki's Heart by Nona j. Moss

Nightmares or Memories by Nona j. Moss

Thought Control by Robert L. Justus

Palightte by James Fly

I, Eugenius by Larry W. Anderson

Tales From Beneath the Crypt by Megan Marie

Vintage Mysteries by Megan Marie

Defenders of Holt by Julie L. Casey

A Thin Strip of Green by Vashti Daise

Fun Activities to Help Little Ones Talk by Kathy Blair

Trade of the Tricks: The Tricks' Brand by David Noe

Tears and Prayers by Harold W. "Doc" Arnett

Thoughts of Mine by Thomas Kirschner

I Am Currency by Whitney L. Grady

Check out these children's titles from
Amazing Things Press

The Boy Who Loved the Sky by Donna E. Hart
Terreben by Donna E. Hart
Sherry Strawberry's Clubhouse by Donna E. Hart
Finally Fall by Donna E. Hart
Thankful for Thanksgiving by Donna E. Hart
Make Room for Maggie by Donna E. Hart
Toddler Tales by Kathy Blair
A Cat Named Phyl by Donna E. Hart
Geography Studies With Animal Buddies by Vashti Daise
The Princess and the Pink Dragon by Thomas Kirschner
Sherry Strawberry's Coloring and Activity Book by Donna E. Hart
The Happy Butterfly by Donna E. Hart
From Seanna by Vashti Daise
The Boy Who Had Nine Cats by Irene Alexander
Meet Mr. Wiggles by Shivonne Jean Hancock
From Seanna Coloring Book by Vashti Daise

Amazing Things Press

www.amazingthingspress.com

Made in the USA
San Bernardino, CA
31 March 2016